CAUGHT!

The eerie stillness of the mountain daybreak seemed all at once magnified. The quail stopped calling on the slope below. The rosy flush of the sun was tipping the Capitáns. Hennepin's voice sounded unnaturally loud to him.

"Maybe we'd ought to have gone with Cuddles. It feels to me as though we might have got a little too close to Soldado's *ranchería* without asking his consent. What you think, Mister Peckinpaugh?"

It was not the old scout who answered, but a deep young voice from the mountainside above and behind them.

"Yes, Mister Peckinpaugh, what do you think?"

The English was very good, and there seemed no anger in the fine bass voice, but the old man shrank visibly.

"Don't move!" he hissed at Hennepin. "That's Soldado."

"That's right," said the Apache chief. "Turn around without your guns."

Will Henry

GHOST WOLF OF THUNDER MOUNTAIN

LEISURE BOOKS   NEW YORK CITY

A LEISURE BOOK®

April 2002

Published by special arrangement with Golden West Literary Agency.

Dorchester Publishing Co., Inc.
276 Fifth Avenue
New York, NY 10001

ISBN 0-8439-4990-2

Printed in the United States of America.

Visit us on the web at www.dorchesterpub.com.

TABLE OF CONTENTS

Acknowledgments

Wolf-Eye

I
"THE BAD ONE"

In the beginning the gray pup had been stamped apart. When one of his small brothers or sisters ventured a playful feint at him, he would return the gesture without any spirit of fun whatsoever. He liked to be aloof and to sit or lie alone and apart. He seemed born with an inherent sense of deep dignity and intense loneliness, and he resented any efforts to invade these feelings.

He was not in any way a savage or vicious puppy, but he was extremely fierce in his demands to be left alone. This, of course, made him a constant center of trouble within the litter. The other puppies, sensing his strangeness, would delight in teasing him into defending his self-appointed kingdom of privacy. Thus it was that before the litter was a month old most of its members bore the marks of the gray one's tiny milk teeth. And thus it was that his owner, shrewd old August Helm, world-famous breeder of German shepherd dogs, was all for doing away with him. The old man knew that such peculiar actions as those of the gray puppy were deep warning signs of a dangerous inheritance, and, while in all the long years of his experience he had never seen one exactly like him, his dog breeder's instinct told him that this puppy should be quietly put to sleep. He would have followed this instinct, and the story of Wolf-Eye would never have been told, if his wife had not talked him out of it.

Two months of hard work ensued for Mrs. Helm as she tried first one thing, then another, in her efforts to make the gray pup behave normally. But the strange forces that were at work within him only strengthened, and the gray one grew steadily worse. For some weeks past he had refused all food except the small portion of raw meat allowed each puppy. Even this he would not eat if anyone were watching. Since his second month he had not barked, and the sounds he made were largely limited to low growls and woofings. Lately he had also taken to whining lonesomely at night, while during the day he paced the length of his run, continuously whimpering and crying nervously.

Old August muttered darkly of "atavisms" and "throwbacks" and "wolf blood," and again insisted the pup be destroyed. His wife would still hear none of his arguments, insisting just as vehemently that the common story of "wolf blood" in the shepherd-dog breed was the sheerest sort of nonsense and that August, of all people, should know it. The old man was forced to agree. Nevertheless, the gray puppy remained just what the Helms would not admit he might be—a throwback to the wolf, in everything save coloration.

In the last regard he was striking. Along his back, from shoulder to haunch, ran a blanket of jet black. The remainder of his body was a soft silver gray, with the fur thick and deep like that of any wild-forest, or range-bred, wolf cub. The rest of his appearance was just as outstanding. Now three months old, he was half again as large as he should have been; he had the bone-work, size, and strength of a five-month puppy. His head was large, and his ears were erect and well-placed. His body was long and low and already muscular to a degree.

But with all his size and beauty of coat, his eyes remained the most vivid feature about him. They were medium-size and almond-shaped and as clear and pale as the finest amber tourmaline. As though in mockery, nature had set them in a black mask. From nose tip to above eye level the face of the gray pup was coal black. In this setting the wild yellow eyes oddly glowed.

Hope for him had finally been abandoned, even by Mrs. Helm, and old August was preparing to destroy him when the kennel had an unexpected visitor. He introduced himself simply as Jim Lewis, a rancher from Arizona. His name, indeed, could have been Jim anything, but his occupation could have been nothing but the one he gave. Nowhere in the world, save on the wind-clean ranges of the American West, has his type been produced.

Of course, the Helms were delighted to show such a visitor through the kennel, especially when it developed he was interested in getting a young puppy to train for the actual herding and working of range cattle. They conducted the rancher immediately to the litter of which the gray pup was a member. This they considered the finest they had to offer.

The gray puppy had, by now, been separated from his mates and had the run adjacent to theirs all to himself. So it was that at first Jim Lewis did not see him. One of the larger pups of the litter, a bold black and tan, had already drawn the rancher's eye and interest. This particular pup chose that very moment to wander up to the wire mesh separating him from his outlawed brother and to hurl a growl of challenge at him.

The black and tan pup had started to turn away from the fence, feeling his challenge had successfully bluffed the gray, when, with a sudden rush of bristling fur, the latter shot out from under his house and toward the fence. The black and tan heard him and wheeled to escape the charge. As he did so, his hip brushed up against the fence. The outcast's teeth flashed through the wire. His brother yelped in pain and leaped away. The gray one scooted back to his hiding place, bringing the whole action to an end less than five seconds from the time it started. But the range-sharpened eye of the lean Arizona rancher had missed nothing.

"I want to see that gray pup," drawled Jim Lewis, nodding toward the solitary one's run. "He looks like a boy that means business."

The Helms tried to brush over the matter, but the rancher knew what he wanted, and finally old August, objecting all the time, dragged out the gray puppy. Once well out in the open, he stood for a moment bewildered; then, noticing the stranger, he crouched low and bared his teeth to the gums.

"Drop the lead," said the rancher quietly. "Let him go."

"But if I do that, he will get away. He'll run immediately," objected old August. "*Himmel!* We would *never* catch him!"

"Go ahead and drop it," ordered Lewis, his voice still easy. "He won't run far."

The instant old August unhooked the leash from the collar, the gray puppy did what the old man thought he would do. He bolted like a crazy thing.

The stranger stepped forward and, making a cup of his hands, pursed his lips and whistled. It was a single, thin, clear whistle, in a peculiar haunting minor key. It made you think at once of lonely places, of sage and pine, piñon and sand, and endless open mesas.

The gray pup checked himself in mid-stride. His haunches shot forward under him, and he came to a skidding stop. Whirling about, he came to rigid attention, his every sense directed to the origin of the whistle. For a moment he held himself thus and then, to the Helms' amazement, uttered a low-pitched, eager whine and took three or four steps back toward the motionless rancher. Now Lewis spoke to him.

"All right, Wolfie. Come on, boy."

In answer to the words the pup moved forward again, not pausing this time until he was directly in front of the towering rancher. The man's size made the puppy look very small and lonely. Neither man nor dog moved.

Then, for the first time in his life, the gray pup wagged his tail slightly. The next minute he was standing up, forepaws on the rancher's leg, and whining softly. He tucked his head apologetically down upon the silver fur of his chest and turned his eyes shyly, hopefully, upward.

"I'll take him," said Jim Lewis.

Plain as they were, those three words were to affect the lives of dozens of humans and countless numbers of animals. They were to prove the biggest words Jim Lewis had ever spoken. But at the moment old August flatly announced that under no circumstances would he allow the "bad one" to go out of the kennel.

Mrs. Helm again proved the guardian of the gray pup's destiny. "Look, Gus! Look how he loves the man already," she said. "See how satisfied he is to be with him. See how quiet he is . . . how steady. Have you ever seen him like this before? Have I? *Nein!*"

Old August growled something under his breath, but what his wife had pointed out was true. The pup was seated at Lewis's feet as calmly and cheerfully as any alley puppy.

Old August could not gainsay the apparent miracle, and so, after some further argument, the gray puppy went away with the Arizona rancher. Old August had seen a thousand puppies come and go, and he was not fooled by this one's sudden attachment to a complete stranger. He was satisfied, in his own mind, that the yellow-eyed puppy had upon him the "stamp of the wolf" and that he could never, no matter what, die a dog's death. All these fears had been put before Jim Lewis, but the big Westerner neither believed nor heeded the old kennel man's insistence that the gray pup was a "bad one."

So it was that the last the Helms saw of the pup he was padding silently along after his new master, looking neither to right nor left but keeping his eyes glued to this long-striding giant of a man to whose services he was now utterly devoted.

II

"WOLF CREEK RANCH"

The Great Mogollon Mesa is the heart of Arizona. It is a wild and lonely region of deep-cleft plateaus, jumbled cañons, and countless minor mesas that will never be anything but sheep and cattle and game country.

Here, on a crisp November morning, came a dilapidated touring car. Jolting and bouncing, it worked its way around the base of Wildcat Mountain. In it were a tall, sun-bronzed man and a sober-faced shepherd puppy.

"Well, this is it, son," chuckled Lewis. "How do you like what you can see of it?"

The pup whined eagerly and thumped the seat with a rapid tattoo of tail beats.

"Name of my place is Wolf Creek," Jim continued. "From here, halfway up old Wildcat Mountain, and over north there clear beyond where you see the water tumblin' out of Wolf Creek, she's all ours."

The pup whined excitedly and emitted a sort of suppressed, happy yap. Then, as though ashamed of his exuberance, he growled and snuggled up to the man's side.

"Don't worry, sonny." The voice was soft. "I have an idea this country and you were made for each other. You'll get along famously." The big man ended his speech with a slow grin and a pat on the pup's head, and once more the shepherd

13

puppy belabored the car seat with happy tail thumps.

The last stretch of the road before the ranch buildings were reached lay through a large pasture called Cedar Flats. It was while driving through this section that the puppy saw his first cattle. The breeding stock on Jim's ranch was the familiar white-faced Herefords, so favored by stockmen the world over. An untold number of these huge red and white animals now startled the roving eye of the shepherd puppy. With a loud snort of amazement he leaped from the car door to Jim's side, and then almost immediately back to the car door again. Hooking his forefeet over the edge, he peered out, completely fascinated.

Jim, who had stopped the car to unbar the gate into the ranch yard, noticing the pup's interest in the white faces, laughed and called to him.

"Take a good look, son. Those fat rascals are your meat, boy. Those are cattle. Cows! You'll see thousands of them before you're through."

The puppy looked at Jim, cocking his head and pitching his ears to hear every word.

"Yeah," Jim went on quietly. "I'm gonna make a herding dog out of you like hasn't been seen in Arizona nor any other place. Right now you'll get a little time to grow up. For the present you can just sorta drift around the ranch and wise yourself up. But remember this"—the rancher wagged his finger under the pup's nose—"time you're a year old, you're gonna be known from one end of the mesa to the other. Yes, sir, my boy! We're gonna show them, sure's your name's. . . ." Jim broke off and looked down, surprised. "Well! Can you tie that? By gosh, we haven't even got a name for you."

The pup wagged his tail and gazed up at the man, his amber eyes glowing with eagerness. Jim studied him. The unblinking regard of the youngster's peculiar eyes drew his attention. In their black-mask setting they shone with particular brilliance. They reminded Jim, suddenly, of the eyes of a big lobo he had trapped the year before. They looked at him in the same way—steadily, thoughtfully, without fear. There was fierceness in them, without treachery. Pride, without egotism. Above all, there was intelligence in every golden glitter of them.

"Wolf-Eye!" said the man suddenly. "That's it. That's your name, son. From now on you're Wolf-Eye."

The rancher drew back and regarded the puppy through half-closed eyes. Yep. That was the name, all right. This pup was the smartest-looking one he had ever seen. And there wasn't any smarter animal in the world than a wolf. Out loud the rancher added, seemingly as an afterthought: "Nor a more cold-blooded one, either."

That night the first crisp finger of winter was laid upon the Mogollons. Wolf-Eye had gone to sleep to a world of color, of gray-green sage and red sandstone. He awoke to a world without color, blanketed from horizon to horizon with two inches of clean snow.

During the preceding day Lewis had wisely allowed the puppy to acquaint himself with the ranch house and yard, and had made no effort to take him about or hurry him in any way. Wolf-Eye had thus spent all day nosing and sniffing around the strange old adobe house and the rambling, Spanish-style, walled-in yard and patio. In this way he came to feel at home immediately.

In twenty-four hours the shy, nervous, skulking creature became an alert, forward, curious youngster. Jim, watching him, felt he could now take him past the yard and introduce him to a little more of the Wolf Creek spread. Further, he had in mind an idea he wanted to try out. So he took down his sheepskin coat from its peg by the kitchen door and, smiling his slow smile, spoke to the waiting Wolf-Eye.

"OK, Wolfie." He had already shortened the formal name to one more easily spoken. "Let's go outdoors. I think this mornin' should really begin your adventures on Wolf Creek Ranch. Yesterday didn't count. You had to look around and take time to forget that you were afraid of everything in the world."

The pup sniffed loudly at the snowy air blowing under the thick oak door. He whined eagerly.

Jim opened the door and went out, holding it for Wolf-Eye to follow. The pup was right behind him. As they stepped off the porch and into the fresh snow, Wolf-Eye trotted along beside the rancher for several steps, and then stopped with a look of sudden and pained concern. Something was very wrong with his feet!

"Snow is the sort of thing nobody can tell you about, Wolfie." Jim laughed. "You have to feel it for yourself. You'll get the hang of it in a minute."

Wolf-Eye looked up at him suspiciously, then lowered his head and snuffed cautiously at the snow blanket. It smelled pretty good. He sniffed again, harder. This time he got his nose full of the powdery snow and sneezed explosively. The force of the sneeze set him back on his haunches. He sat there in the snow a moment, a puzzled look on his face, then leaped to his feet and stood looking at his rear in great wonder. It was burning like fire!

He inspected the snow where he had been sitting. No sign of heat there. Strange! He was sure he'd had his rear singed there a moment before. What kind of country was this, anyway? A fellow couldn't even sit down in comfort. The burning left his rear and returned to his feet. He began to pick them up and set them down so rapidly that he was soon doing a peculiar, four-footed jig.

Jim, who had gone on ahead, laughed and called to him across the yard. The pup looked at him, hesitated, then took off across the snow like a thing possessed. As he ran, the burn left his feet, and the cold snowy air felt fresh and good in his nostrils. In a moment he was rolling and tumbling and rooting up the snow and plowing along through it, biting, clawing, growling, and snapping. Reaching Jim, he jumped and flung himself upon him, pawing and nipping at his boots and trouser legs; rolling over and over in the snow; scampering crazily about, slipping, falling, sprawling, at last coming to a panting rest at the rancher's feet. His plumy tail swept the snow rapidly, and his heavy panting split his face in a toothy grin. It was a rare display of emotion.

"Now, Wolfie," said Jim, "we're gonna educate you to the horse. The horse is a creature different from the cow as day is from night, but you have to know just as much about him as you do them, to be around where cattle are bein' handled."

As he spoke, Jim was letting down the poles of a small horse corral in which the home ranch saddle stock was kept. As he repeated the word horse, he pointed at the ponies within the enclosure, but Wolf-Eye hung back and peered suspiciously at the half dozen queer creatures trotting and shifting around.

They were an odd lot, all right—and smelled entirely different from the big red and white cows. These creatures had long hair on their necks and rears, and they moved and pranced around much faster than the red and white ones.

Jim quickly roped and saddled a stocking-footed bay and led him out of the corral. Wolf-Eye, who had been watching all the action with great interest, now came forward and stretched out his muzzle for a tentative sniff at the hind hoof of the big brown creature his master was holding. Jim said nothing, although he knew what was about to happen. He had his own theories on the training of dogs, and one of them was that experience trains the fastest.

As Wolf-Eye's nose neared the horse's hoof, the bay suddenly tensed his hindquarters and shot a short, sharp kick at the puppy's head. Wolf-Eye, with that wonderfully acute warning instinct that was to serve him so well in the future, sensed his danger the moment the horse tightened his quarters. Thus he had already started to draw back when the hoof whizzed at him. As a result he got only a grazing tip on the shoulder and was not injured, but only tumbled over and banged up against a fence post. He scrambled to his feet, limped off a way, and sat down to consider the situation. Squinting speculatively at the corral, he made a mental note to stay away from the hind hoofs of horses from that time on.

"Sorry, old-timer," drawled Jim, wagging his head. "But horses are like snow. You have to feel them yourself to know what they're like. There's nothin' about gettin' kicked that anybody can describe better than a horse."

The puppy looked at him a little resentfully.

Jim chuckled. "Now don't get peeved, Wolfie. If I'd have tried to tell you about a horse, you wouldn't have paid any attention. But when a horse tells you about a horse, that's different. You pay attention. And you remember."

Jim was right. Wolf-Eye was never again kicked by a horse. In addition to fine instincts, he possessed a huge and faithful memory. He never forgot anything, good or bad, that happened to him. This faculty, too, was to play an important part in the adventure that lay ahead of him.

But now his tall idol was doing a strange thing. He was actually climbing up on that brown beast, and the two of them were starting off through the snow toward the hills in back of the ranch buildings. Losing no time, Wolf-Eye galloped after them. Giving the horse plenty of room, he fell into a wobbly puppy trot that managed to keep him fairly well abreast of Jim and his mount.

Noticing his ungainly efforts to keep up, the horseman grinned down at him and said: "This is plumb normal, Wolfie. This is the way we get around in this country. And, incidentally, pay attention, because you're gettin' your first lesson . . . how to follow a man on horseback. It's not as easy as it looks. It takes a lot of breath and quite a little brains."

Wolf-Eye wasn't long in finding this out. At first, he could keep up pretty well, but, what with an occasional piece of deep snow, or a small dry wash, or a steep spot on a hillside, he was soon far behind.

Looking back, Jim felt his throat muscles tighten. The pup was certainly no quitter. He was really working to keep up. He watched the small gray figure as it fell farther and farther behind, expecting at any minute to hear Wolf-Eye yelp or cry out. But no sound came from the struggling puppy.

"Well, now, we'll see what the little cuss can really do," muttered Jim half aloud, and, putting the spurs to the bay, he set off a pace that soon left Wolf-Eye completely out of sight.

Doubling back around a big, low hill, the horseman headed for the ranch buildings, after putting a good mile between himself and the trailing puppy. Once at the ranch, he unsaddled the bay and sat down on the corral fence to await the outcome of his experiment.

He had a good reason for this test, for running away from the puppy, deserting him, leaving him on his own. This might appear to be a simple sort of test and one that the puppy might solve any way he saw fit, without disgracing himself. But the way Wolf-Eye worked it out would tell Jim a lot about what kind of brain lay behind those slanting golden eyes, what kind of heart beat in the deep chest. He was not long in getting his answer.

A few minutes after he returned, he made out the puppy's small form coming around the base of the low hill—and coming around the right side of it. He was moving at a good gait but not hurrying or panicky. He was traveling nose-down, and running out the horse's trail as though he had been trained for a lifetime to do nothing else. When he finally came up panting to Jim's feet, he had hardly the strength to fall down. Nevertheless, his black muzzle was split wide in that toothy grin Jim would come to know so well, and his yellow eyes were fairly sparkling with pride.

Jim had gotten the answer he wanted.

He reached down and picked the shepherd puppy up in his arms and carried him into the ranch house as carefully as a baby. Inside, he took off his sheepskin and threw it on the bed, then lowered Wolf-Eye onto it. The puppy was tired, worn out. He was asleep before Jim put him down.

III
"UNWELCOME GUEST"

Daily now, Jim took the swiftly growing shepherd puppy on long rides across the great ranch. However, Wolf-Eye had not yet met any of the cowboys and handy men employed by Lewis. They had been out in the different cow camps, working the fall roundup, when Wolf-Eye came to the ranch. He met them all in good time, but his first introduction was to old Juan Garcia, Jim's Mexican roundup cook. The way this meeting took place furnished a pretty good indication of the shepherd's expanding sense of importance. He had moved in at Wolf Creek Ranch, and his reception of the unsuspecting Mexican proved the point to everyone's satisfaction—except, perhaps, Juan's!

Juan had run out of coffee at the roundup camp and had driven to the home ranch late one night to stock up again. He had not the faintest suspicion that *el patrón* had acquired a new dog.

Not wishing to awaken his employer at such a late hour, the old Mexican tiptoed across the ranch yard and eased the kitchen door gently open, meaning to get his supplies and leave without disturbing *el patrón*. All this might have come off as planned, except that, as he crept across the moonlit yard, a pair of slanted yellow eyes followed his every step.

Quietly Wolf-Eye had eased himself down off the foot of Jim's bed. With a quick movement he had slipped through

21

the half open door into the hall and padded along the tile floor to the kitchen. As he came into the room, Garcia was just fumbling the latch on the outside door. There was not a sound save that made by the old man at the door.

In a moment, though, there was sound to spare. As the door opened, Wolf-Eye could see the black shape of a man framed against the moonlight. That was all he needed. With a quick rush he made for the intruder.

Old Juan had just struck a light as Wolf-Eye started his rush. The first thing the Mexican saw was a savage-looking gray beast with blazing yellow eyes—and the beast was roaring at him. With a scream of terror the old man wheeled about and raced for his chuck wagon.

About three jumps short of the safety of the wagon, Wolf-Eye's teeth met in the seat of old Juan's blue denims. The fear-crazed Mexican continued his flight without the benefit of pants. The team of ponies, not recognizing their master without his drawers, took alarm and bolted. Old Juan barely managed to make a flying leap for the tailgate of the wagon as it swept past him.

To add to the occasion Wolf-Eye gave the near horse a neat slash in the hock. This caused the animal to leap sideways into his running mate, thus fouling the harness and tripping both horses to the ground in a kicking, squealing mess. Contributing its bit to the general mêlée, the wagon tongue cracked off short and the chuck wagon went staggering onto its side, spilling dried beans, flour, sugar, salt, and part of a quarter of beef all over the yard. For a moment Wolf-Eye surveyed the wreckage, then trotted proudly back toward the kitchen door with the south part of Juan's pants clenched firmly in his jaws.

By this time Jim was out in the yard in his nightshirt with a Coleman lantern held high. Having recognized old Juan's

Latin yells, he called out for the Mexican to make known his whereabouts. The horses had now regained their composure and were standing quietly, but the cook was nowhere to be seen.

Eventually Jim dug him out of the flour sacks and bean bags still within the overturned wagon, but no amount of argument would induce the old man to leave his sanctuary until Wolf-Eye had been closed up in the house. Only then did he come forth and listen to *el patrón*'s explanations of the wolf in the house.

Thus it was that the first news which the men in the camp got of Wolf-Eye came from the disgruntled Mexican cook. It wasn't a particularly good beginning for the big puppy. Cowboys are little less superstitious than sailors, and, while most of them got a good laugh at the remains of Juan's pants, several of them listened with nodding heads while the old Mexican cursed the shepherd dog. No good could come from a wolf dog in stock country. That much was certain.

When they finally got around to knowing him, most of the men forgot all about the dog, or at least disdained him. Wolf-Eye didn't court attention. His newly found belief in Jim did not take in the rest of humanity. The men, to him, were still strangers and would always remain so. When they made overtures to him, he ignored them completely. Very few things sit so poorly with a man as to have a dog turn him down, so in the end the men left the shepherd alone. Lewis, sensing the resentment they felt for the dog, wisely said nothing of his plans to make a cow herder out of him.

Nonetheless, as he turned six months, Wolf-Eye's serious schooling with cattle began. Jim worked him in solitude, and the men knew nothing of the young dog's training.

IV

"MARK OF THE WOLF"

Through the brief winter Wolf-Eye grew enormously. At nine months he weighed more than one hundred pounds and stood well above a tall man's knee in height. And Jim had him beautifully trained. In fact, Sunday cow herding exhibitions had become a fixture at Wolf Creek Ranch. Neighboring cattlemen rode in from all over the mesa to watch the pup work cattle.

Most of the visitors had herding dogs of their own, trained on sheep for the most part but capable of handling a handful of cattle in a pinch. Still, to a man, they allowed they'd never seen the beat of Jim's dog for handling beef stock.

Jim controlled Wolf-Eye with whistles and hand signals. The only time his owner used his voice in the herding work was at the beginning of any task, when he would use the single, rousing cry—"Hi . . . Wolf-Eye!"—to rivet the dog's attention to the fact that work was to be done, and at the conclusion of the work, when he would say simply: "Good dog, Wolfie. Good dog."

Strangely enough, through all this period of excitement over him, none of his admirers had marked a peculiarity of the big German shepherd's eyes—or, if they had, none of them had said anything about it. Certainly there had been no wolf talk prior to the last exhibition at Wolf Creek Ranch. For this exhibition Jim had gone out to his west range and scoured the gullies and arroyos thoroughly. The result had been a dozen old mossbacks, proddy and salty enough to satisfy the most doubting taste. Three- and four-year-old steers they were, raw-boned, spooky-eyed devils that would easily average twelve hundred pounds. A few of the older hands present doubted that Wolf-Eye would be able to "put these babies in."

The routine through which the rancher and Wolf-Eye were to go consisted of five main steps. Collection of the scattered cattle. Bunching and holding them at the branding chute. Sending them into the chute one at a time, meanwhile holding the rest of them in a compact bunch. Picking up each steer at the release end of the chute and returning it to the held group. Driving the branded group into the holding pen and keeping them there until relieved.

Wolf-Eye was facing his baptism of fire. Yet he showed no hesitancy.

The first step in the routine was the prettiest, from the spectators' viewpoint. In preparation, several ranchers had run the big steers up into the gully-washed hills back of the ranch. In ten minutes there wasn't hide or hair of the twelve beasts showing.

It now became Wolf-Eye's job to go out and find his cattle. The audience was ready. Those who had ridden over on horseback remained mounted to help out in any emergency. The others, including quite a few women and children, peered from buggy or buckboard, or adorned the various corral fences. Nobody was afoot for the reason that afoot was no place to be, what with a dozen spooked-up steers running around.

Finally Jim ordered out the gray pup. Belly down and racing easily, Wolf-Eye moved toward the hills. He was out of sight in an instant but immediately reappeared, driving two of the missing steers ahead of him. Before his audience could settle back, he had collected seven of the scattered animals and jumped four of the remaining five. With the group numbering eleven he started for the ranch. A murmur arose from the watchers—the pup was one steer short.

But Wolf-Eye made the count almost as quickly as they did. With a rush he sent the cattle down the hillside in a gallop. Then he doubled back up the slope, quartering through the heavy sage like a bird dog on quail, exactly the way Jim had taught him. Suddenly he turned in mid-stride and dived over the bank of a brush-covered gully. A second later he came flashing out again. Ahead of him, tail up and eyes rolling, plunged the missing steer, a big, high-shouldered, brindle rascal whose humped withers and scimitar-shaped horns gave evidence of Brahma blood.

The other cattle bawled in surprise and fell apart to let the big red steer through, then reformed in his wake. A cheer arose from the group around the corrals. Not a man there but knew it would have been impossible for a man on horseback to duplicate that feat—for that matter, not three or four men. Jim's experiment was well begun.

As the puppy drew near with his charges, Jim spurred over to a spot by the branding chute. Wolf-Eye moved out from behind the cattle and watched his owner. Jim whistled and dropped his hand toward the ground, indicating the spot over which he and the horse stood. It was the checking signal. He was showing Wolf-Eye where he wanted the cattle stopped.

Wolf-Eye disappeared, and instantly the herd shifted its course and moved for the spot the rancher had marked. The spectators applauded and yelled. Then another shout of appreciation went up as Wolf-Eye brought the bawling herd to a stop. Quickly he turned the leaders, snapping at the heels of the laggards. In a moment the bunch was milling nicely, precisely over the ground Jim had pointed out.

The tall rancher raised his hand, then passed it in a diagonal movement down and across his body—the cutting signal.

Wolf-Eye selected a big dun steer and cut him out. Moving the creature from the herd to the branding chute was the work of a moment. To complete the show Jim locked the steer in the chute and rammed an unheated iron into his flank, then released him. As he burst from the chute exit, Wolf-Eye was there to pick him up and turn him back to the herd. Jim signaled another cut, and the dog started the second steer for the chute. Again and again the cut was made, until all but one of the steers had been run in and branded.

This steer was the one that had hidden out on Wolf-Eye. He was a salty old devil, range-wise from several undisturbed seasons in the open—one of those occasional mossbacks that through a superior gift of craft manages consistently to slip through the roundup gathers and remains at liberty. Now he cautiously circled, keeping his widespread horns always in the dog's direction, never allowing him to get behind him.

Wolf-Eye made two attempts to get in at the old warrior. Each time he was nearly gored for his trouble, the second time so closely that the sweeping horn parted his thick fur. The dog was puzzled. He hesitated, looked across at Jim.

"What does he do now, Jim?" The voice was mocking. "Send for the nearest cowhand?"

"Naw," another deriding spectator answered. "He borrows Jim's rope and slaps a loop on the critter."

"Sure," chimed in a third. "Then he drags him over to the chute and tows him right on in!"

Jim, ignoring the good-natured comments, called to the waiting puppy: "Easy, boy. Easy."

This was a time of real crisis for the young dog, and the

rancher waited a moment for him to relax. Wolf-Eye looked at Jim, drew off from the steer a bit, then looked at his master again.

Jim knew it was now or never. "Hi . . . Wolf-Eye!" he said sharply.

The gray dog seemed to stiffen at the words. A low growl came from his throat. The hair on his back began to lift. He again faced the belligerent steer.

"Go on in and get him," Jim said quietly. There was no sound from the spectators, and the words carried clearly to the waiting dog.

Wolf-Eye began to move in slowly. The steer looked up puzzled, then lowered his head and backed off. Still the pup came on, his yellow eyes holding the steer's red ones, his feet treading as daintily as a cat's. The Brahma blew through his nostrils, pawed angrily. Wolf-Eye came on. He was almost up to the beast.

The steer charged without warning. Wolf-Eye leaped aside, and the murderous animal thundered by harmlessly. Before he could check his speed, Wolf-Eye was behind him—behind him and driving him like a gray fury.

Just short of the chute the wily old Brahma made an attempt to turn out. Wolf-Eye hit his flank like a thunderbolt, and the big brindle turned squarely into the chute. Accompanied by a cheer from the crowd and a hearty—"Good dog, Wolfie. Good dog!"—from his master, Wolf-Eye headed the brindle back toward the herd as Jim quickly released him from the chute. In a moment he had the entire bunch milling, and then, in another moment, heading for the holding pen. The cattle were tired, moving obediently. Only the big brindle lagged behind and kept a wary eye on the dog. It was apparent the show was over. Those big tough beeves were going to amble into the holding pen like moo cows into a milking shed. The applause was loud and long—but premature.

The steers were all in the holding pen, and Wolf-Eye stood barring the exit when it happened. Jim, contrary to his custom of riding up on horseback to close the gate, dismounted and walked over. It was one of those unreasonable things people are forever doing on the spur of the moment, only to wonder later what they could have been thinking of.

The brindle steer, already beside himself with rage, was at the breaking point of his natural fear of the dog. All that held him was the cold, watchful eye of the wolf-like figure, crouched in the open gateway. Wolf-Eye, hearing Jim's footsteps, turned for an instant to see what was wrong, why his master should be afoot. At the same instant the big brindle spotted the approaching rancher. To a steer on prod, a man on foot means just one thing. With a harsh bellow the creature charged.

Jim, seeing him start, ran for the nearest fence. Several of the ranchers spurred forward to head the steer off. They were too late—could never have made it. And then from nowhere appeared the raging figure of Wolf-Eye.

The action was too fast and dust-clouded to be seen, but it appeared the dog must have gone in under the steer's feet and tripped him, for the big Brahma went suddenly up in the air and fell on his side with a bone-shattering crunch. He kicked violently for a brief moment, then lay still. There wasn't a sound from the spectators.

"Well," announced Jim breathlessly. "Acts like he was plumb bored with trippin' up twelve-hundred-pound steers."

" 'Pears that way," agreed another. " 'Course, if Jim had got himself killed, old Poker Face might've stopped long enough to give him a quick lick. But just look at him now, will you?"

They all turned as the speaker pointed. Wolf-Eye was back at his post, standing in the middle of the holding pen's gateway. Not a steer had escaped from the pen. The dog was back on the job. A murmur ran round the crowd. Talk about your working dogs! Good Christmas!

Jim came up to the puppy and without a word swung the gate shut. "Good dog, Wolfie," he said. "Good dog."

The relief in the dog was visible. He reared up and placed his forepaws on Jim's chest, muzzling the rancher's cheek softly. Jim put his arms around the furry neck. Words at this time would have meant nothing. Wolf-Eye probably didn't understand the moment or, for that matter, did most of the hardened stockmen present. But one thing was certain. There wasn't a dry eye within twenty miles of Wolf Creek, and lumps in the throat could have been had for ten cents a dozen.

In the midst of this awkward situation there came an interruption. "Holy sufferin' smokes!" a voice exploded. "Good gosh!" It was Clay Peters, standing over by the carcass of the Brahma steer. The old man straightened up from his inspection of the dead animal. "Jim!" he called, and his voice carried strangely in the silence. "Come over here a minute, will you? The rest of you boys, too."

"Comin', Clay," responded Jim, moving over toward the cattleman.

As the young rancher approached, the old man drawled slowly: "Take a look at this critter's neck and then tell me somethin'." The old rancher's tones went suddenly flat as he concluded: "Take a *good* look at it."

Jim squatted to examine the dead steer.

The old man's voice rasped on. "I figured his neck was broken by that fall he took from the dog trippin' him up. Same as the rest of you," he challenged the gathering ranchers. "But it wasn't. It wasn't no more broke than nothin'. And, furthermore, he wasn't more tripped than nothin'." The men were silent, listening, as the old man concluded: "That there critter's throat is sliced open from ear to ear. There's half a foot of his windpipe hangin' out!"

The ranchers looked at Jim. Slowly the owner of the Wolf Creek spread came to his feet. The muscles in his jaw worked. Extending his booted foot, he turned the steer's head. It rolled to one side, sagging at a grotesque angle. A murmur of disbelief ran through the crowding ranchers. From ear to ear, and as cleanly as though done with a stock knife, the steer's throat was laid open.

Black blood dripped from the wound. There was a pause during which no one moved or spoke. Then old man Peters announced thoughtfully: "In forty years I've never seen a dog cut a throat like that."

There were no answers. The deed was its own dark indictment. The mark of the wolf was on the silent carcass. Each of the ranchers realized it; all were to have cause to remember it. Quietly the men walked off, singly and in groups. Finally Jim stood alone by the stiffening carcass.

V

"VOICES IN THE WIND"

Roundup time at Wolf Creek was a season of heavy work. Jim was running three thousand head, and this meant close to nine hundred calves to be cut out and branded. The work was grist to Wolf-Eye's mill. He learned more about cattle in thirty days than the average herd dog learns in a lifetime. Even the noncommittal 'punchers were forced to admit that the dog was no slouch.

He was especially good in the calf branding. In this work the cows with new calves were held in a group while the 'punchers cut out the calves one at a time and dragged them, kicking and bellowing, to the branding fire. During this business the old cows would get excited. Their instinct called for instant battle in defense of their bellowing young. So nearly every calf roped would be followed out of the herd by a thousand pounds of outraged mother cow intent on killing herself a cowpuncher. When run back into the herd by other 'punchers, the old cows would try again and again to escape and follow their calves.

This constant charging out of the herd and down upon the men at the fire represented real danger to them. It was in the touch-and-go action of protecting these men at the fire that Wolf-Eye excelled. He seemed to be everywhere at once, ranging the front of the herd like a shadow. If an old cow poked her nose out of line, Wolf-Eye was there to nip it back for her. If a head were lowered for the charge, he was there to dive under it and snap wickedly to force it back up again.

At first, some of the cows refused to be intimidated by the gray dog's rushing and snapping. These quickly learned. There were no punches pulled once an animal had been warned. The whole herd sensed the fact that here was a new and sterner authority than it had ever known before.

If Wolf-Eye needed a clincher to his command of the situation, it was supplied by an old cow that had the bad judgment to try a charge behind his back. Hearing the quick, dry rattle of the creature's hoofs on the ground, he spun around to intercept her. Straight in under her he drove, throwing his shoulder into her forelegs and knocking them cleanly out from under the speeding animal. She rolled head over heels and came to earth with a jarring crash. Wolf-Eye rolled clear, and in a moment the shaken cow got awkwardly to her feet and limped back to the herd. The men at the fire gave the big gray puppy a half laugh, half cheer of commendation. The dog waved his plumed tail in rare gratitude and trotted proudly back to his post.

Before long the last calf for the day was handled and the quick western twilight came off the shoulder of Wildcat Mountain like a purple curtain. The cook's fires were treating the surrounding mesa to the pleasant aroma of broiling steaks, and the coyotes were beginning to tune up over by Wolf Creek Pass. The roundup crew lingered over the last cup of old Juan Garcia's coffee and talked over the day's work. To a man the 'punchers swore they had never seen the beat of Wolf-Eye's handling of the old cow. Graciously they allowed the big shepherd had his spurs coming for his performance that day.

The roundup passed and summer lengthened over the Mogollons. The pace of work lessened, and Wolf-Eye had many hours to himself. These were the deep hours of midnight, the gray hours of the dawn. These were the hours when the dog listened to the voices in the wind and sampled with his delicate nostrils the news in the air. This was the wind that came gliding over the low tops of the Black Hills laden with the smell of the ptarmigan, sage hen, and quail, of the mule deer, big-horn sheep, and coyote. And this was the wind that came leaping down from the snows of Wildcat Mountain heavy with smells that lifted the hairs of the back—smells of the black bear, the mountain lion, and the timber wolf!

Wolf-Eye smelled this wind and listened to it. It made him uncomfortable, lonesome. He whimpered and moved about the ranch nervously. This restlessness did not escape Jim. To his wilderness-wise eyes it was no great secret what was troubling the dog. These days were the forerunners of the wild creatures' mating season. Fall was drawing into mid-November, the frosts were becoming regular, and the moon was filling. Life and action and love were all abroad in the crisp wind. Wolf-Eye was past his first year now, and he knew the spell of these things; that is, he *felt* it. And the feeling grew stronger with each passing day. This was the time and the place to fix the great dog's future.

Jim knew it. Either the dog in Wolf-Eye would ascend now or the wolf would predominate. And that would be the end of it. If old August Helm's dire forecast for Wolf-Eye's future were the true one, these were the days that would prove it. These were the days and these were the nights to fight for Wolf-Eye's allegiance. Would the man win or would the wilderness? Could Jim hold the dog against the spell of the outer mesa? What chance did the rancher have against the wild voices that came to Wolf-Eye on the wind? One thing was certain. In this game the first chance was the last one!

The tall owner of Wolf Creek Ranch worked hard to hold his faithful shadow to him. To Jim, watching the gray shepherd struggle with the urges within him, it was not like watching a dog reacting to the common, ordinary urge to run off into the wild—but most like seeing a dear friend, the best friend in the whole world, getting sicker and sicker and not being able to do anything to help him.

However, watching and working were the only things Jim could do to help Wolf-Eye now. Nights were the bad times, and for the present the big dog was allowed to return to his old place on the foot of Jim's bed. Here his master could quiet him when he became restless, and speak to him reassuringly when he whimpered or moved about. Wolf-Eye's bed beneath the stunted cedar in the yard became weed-grown from disuse.

For a time things went well. As the season progressed, Wolf-Eye quieted down. His appetite picked up. Jim's routine of work and watchfulness appeared to be having the desired effect. Although he didn't relax his vigilance, the rancher began to feel the battle was nearly over. This satisfaction was well and good as far as it went. But it didn't go far enough. It didn't go nearly so far as to include the soft-footed form of Vega, the she-wolf!

Jim had just finished unsaddling the bay, after having ridden a twenty-mile swing out around Wolf Creek Pass for the purpose of tiring Wolf-Eye. Giving the sweaty pony a quick rub-off with a handful of hay, the rancher leaned against the corral fence and rolled a smoke. Twilight had already passed, and a lopsided three-quarter moon was overhead. Wolf-Eye squatted by his master's side, his pink tongue lolling out, his yellow eyes peering up at Jim through the heavy dusk. He listened with interest as Jim talked of supper.

"How about some chuck, Wolfie? It wouldn't surprise me if you really ate tonight. Old Bay and I sure wore you down, didn't we? Twenty miles at a trot is enough to discourage any-body's romantic tendencies. You won't be lyin' awake to-night worryin' about any excursions into the brush."

The big shepherd growled deeply in his throat—a special, satisfied growl that he reserved for occasions like this when he was happy—and the two turned to enter the ranch house. As they did so, a voice boomed out of the gathering dark.

"Hey, Jim! That you? Wait up a minute. I got some mail for you."

Recognizing old Clay Peters, Jim called back: "Howdy, Clay. Get down and come in. We were just gonna get us some grub together."

"No, thanks, Jim." The old man's voice was tired. "Gotta be gettin' on. Ain't fed the calves yet." As he spoke, he handed Jim the mail.

"Well, all right, Clay. Much obliged."

"Nothin' to it. Glad to do it." The old man turned his pony away. Suddenly he yelled: "Whoa thar, blast you!"

Jim could hardly make out the pitching form of the pinto saddle mare. "Reckon we'll hafta get you a gas buggy right soon, Clay," he called obligingly. "You can't hold your seat like you used to."

"Balls o' fire!" the old rancher roared. "This here paint hoss ain't reared on me in ten years. I broke her from a suckin' colt. She seen somethin' she don't like, I tell ya. She ain't no darn' fool cow horse. Now what do ya suppose got to eatin' her? Maybe it was . . . ah, ha!" The old man broke off triumphantly. "I told ya, by gosh! It's that dang wolf dog of yores!"

"Sorry, Clay," Jim chuckled. "Reckon Old Paint don't cotton to dogs."

"I'll take leave of ya on that, Jim Lewis," cried the old man indignantly. "This here pony's been around dogs all her life. She ain't never shied at no *dog* before."

Jim ignored the emphasis. "Well, don't worry none, Clay," he soothed. "Wolf-Eye's plumb gentle. He won't bother your pony. There isn't a mean hair in him."

"Maybe." The bitter tones drifted back out of the darkness. "Maybe. But I'm still sayin' Old Paint was brung up with dogs 'n' she ain't never paid 'em no heed. You can call that beast of yours a dog, if you've a mind to, but me, I got my own name for him . . . 'n' it ain't *dog!*"

Jim stood staring into the night for several seconds. Off on the south range a coyote yapped. Another answered from the direction of Portal Rocks. The rancher sighed. "I'm sure havin' a time sellin' you to these old mossbacks around here, Wolfie."

The dog reared and placed his forepaws on the rancher's shoulders.

"You're just a poor, big, overgrown moose," Jim mused. "Haven't got a friend in the world, have you?"

Wolf-Eye pressed closer and shoved his cold nose against the man's ear.

"Sure, boy," the rancher muttered. "You stick close to me and you won't need any other friends."

Wolf-Eye followed his master into the house. He moved by his knee, never taking his eyes from him. Like golden mirrors they reflected every motion the rancher made. But unlike mirrors they reflected more than movement. In them was worship, mysterious and all-inclusive—the kind of worship only a dog can give a man.

After supper Jim went outside for a final smoke before turning in. Wolf-Eye followed him. The man's big brown hand rumpled the thick fur of the dog's neck, scratched slowly under his powerful paw. These were the times Wolf-Eye lived for. These were his minutes—his peace and contentment. He stretched gratefully under the caress of the thoughtful hand. A deep rumble of satisfaction shook his chest. He whined and reached a searching paw for his master's knee.

Presently Jim flipped away his cigarette. "Come on, boy," he yawned. "Let's turn in. Another day tomorrow."

In twenty minutes the house was quiet. Wolf-Eye lay in his accustomed spot at the foot of Jim's bed. From the rancher came the regular breathing of deep sleep. The dog's sense of security began to dissipate, as it always did when a man deserted him in sleep. He stirred restlessly, soon arose, and padded over to the open window. In a moment he leaped to the thick adobe sill, hesitated, then dropped to the ground outside. Circling, he bedded down under his cedar tree.

Suddenly something aroused him. He came to his feet nervously, looked about him. There was nothing. What could it have been? Something had awakened him. What was it?

A great feeling of loneliness seized him. A deep surge of primal feeling welled up in him. Throwing back his head, he howled—once, twice, three times. Then he fell silent, listening. From afar and high above came an answering howl, high, thin, musical.

VI

"LOTHAR, THE WOLF"

Vega, the she-wolf, had been an orphan cub. Born two springs ago on the naked shoulder of Wildcat Mountain, she had known a mother's milk but six short weeks. Then distemper, the White Plague of the wilderness, had snuffed out not only the old she-wolf's life but the lives of four of her five cubs. Vega, the fifth cub, had remained whimpering in the filth of the death den for several days. Finally, driven by hunger, she had sought the outer world.

And a strange world it was. To the shivering wolf cub, it was full of frightening noises and shapes. It proved a world of glorious warmth by day, of bitter cold by night. How the tottering, malnourished cub survived remains one of nature's peculiar secrets.

Now in the third month of her second year, Vega was a thing of beauty. Her color and markings were unique. Light creamy fawn was her body color, with the legs and belly parts shading to near white. Down her neck and rearward to midtail ran a deep over coloring of clear auburn red. The manner in which this blended with her undercoat gave her a definite coppery-red cast. Her face markings were typically those of a wolf—a mask of creamy white darkening to shadowy gray above the eyes.

In the full of her second mating season Vega felt the call of love. Softly she came treading around the shoulder of Wildcat

Mountain. Downward she glided, every sense on the alert. The mating moon hung low in the midnight sky. Far below, at the foot of Wildcat, twinkled the lights of Wolf Creek Ranch. The she-wolf paused and gazed down. A lull fell in the wind. Vega stiffened and swung her ears to the lights below. Across the miles of still air drifted a long, lonesome howl. Again it came, low-pitched and sad.

Every hair on the she-wolf's back vibrated on end. A yellow froth flecked her lips. Her jaws quivered and chopped. A third time now the call quavered across the miles.

Straightening, the she-wolf flung her muzzle heavenward. Her lips parted. From them came a high-pitched whine— more of a wail it was, actually—that echoed down the mountainside, down even to Cedar Flats and across them, even among the very buildings of Wolf Creek Ranch itself. Jim heard it and came upright in bed. Another instant and he was running for the door. Outside, his calls for Wolf-Eye went unanswered. The dog was gone.

The big rancher twisted his lips bitterly. He should have known better. He should have known he couldn't beat the spell of the mesa. He should have known that when the call really came, when love actually sent for Wolf-Eye, the dog would go. Jim knew the howl of a she-wolf as well as he knew the bawl of a calf. And he knew what he had to do, now that the dog was gone.

He went into the house and dressed. Then, making a pack, he got his rifle from the rack above the mantel. Snapping open the breech of the stubby Winchester, he grunted with satisfaction as the gleaming cartridge flipped out.

As Jim set off across Wolf Creek Meadow, the light of the waning moon was good. It made the big dog's line of tracks as clear as a buffalo trail. It glimmered on the black barrel of the Winchester slung across the rancher's back.

* * * * *

Jim was not the only interested party besides Wolf-Eye to hear Vega's call. Lothar, the old wolf, heard it.

All season Lothar had sought a mate, but females were scarce. The distemper had taken a heavy toll among the wolves. For eight seasons Lothar had mated in the Mogollons. Many were the sturdy sons and slim daughters of his siring that coursed these hills. In all the region no wolf dared stand before Lothar. His power on the mesa went undisputed. And never before had the old wolf gone mateless. Now the season was beginning and no soft female trotted by his side.

Belly down, Wolf-Eye slunk across the open to Wolf Creek Meadow. Within the shadows of Cedar Flats he lengthened his stride. When the rolling aprons of Wildcat Mountain passed beneath him, he was going in the long trot that is the trail gait of the wolf. Behind him the calls of Jim Lewis were lost in another world.

In a moon-silver clearing high above Wolf Creek the great dog halted. From above him and to the right he heard the clear notes of Vega's call. It was close and ran through him like an electric shock. It lifted every hair on his spine, left his jaws champing crazily. He didn't answer the she-wolf but disappeared in the direction of her call like a puff of gray smoke. Soon he was close beneath the timberline. Here the trees grew stunted and far apart, and his breath came painfully short.

Wolf-Eye paused to regain his wind. He peered about. The female was somewhere close at hand, possibly within a few feet. Puzzled, he circled about.

Then the moon slid around the shoulder of Wildcat Mountain. He started. There she was, not a hundred feet away! Still as a statue, slender profile to the moon. Wolf-Eye stood enchanted.

Suddenly he sank to the ground, ears forward, every sense strained to a point about twenty paces below the slim young female. The she-wolf caught the disturbance, also. She swung her head in its direction. From beneath the black screen of the hemlocks crept the squat figure of Lothar. Vega watched him, fascinated. Wolf-Eye crouched motionless.

Nose to nose Lothar stood with the she-wolf, his bushy tail waving slowly. The young female was trembling.

Wolf-Eye, too, was upset. In the dry grasses of his hiding place he shook as from a sudden fit. Then, as the old wolf's overtures to the female progressed, he became angry. But this anger died very suddenly. Wolf-Eye was conscious for the first time of the power in the old wolf's frame, of the flat snakiness of his skull, the length of his powerful jaws. The big shepherd was afraid. Shamelessly he turned and fled.

Nature conspired to redeem him. In his haste he failed to see a pile of loose stones. In a moment he tripped and fell, sprawling. In the stillness a deaf one could have heard the noise at a hundred paces.

Instantly Lothar's eyes swept to the struggling dog. Shortly Wolf-Eye kicked himself clear of the tumbling rocks and stood revealed in the moonlight. His general size and shape were wolfish, and Lothar surmised he had an impudent young wolf rival to deal with. Here, apparently, was some upstart who had not heard of Lothar. Ordinarily he would have dismissed such a one with a couple of threatening snarls, but this one was big, and quite handsome. Finishing him off might impress the female.

As if to convince himself the prize was worth the exercise, Lothar studied the young female. She was a beauty. In his eight seasons he had not seen one worthy to lick the snow-ice from between her footpads. Yes, here was something worth impressing. Haughtily Lothar started across the clearing.

Wolf-Eye watched the wolf come. Strangely there was no fear in his heart now. As he looked at the red female, all the wild emotions of the earlier part of the evening returned. Each hair of his roach stood and quivered with individual life. His frame tensed, and the muscles rolled and set beneath his heavy coat. His eyes bored across the clearing and locked with those of the she-wolf, remained so locked for one thrilling moment. Then Lothar charged.

Wolf-Eye's hindquarters rose beneath him, propelling him outward into the clearing and into full charge. From his throat burst a bellowing challenge. With the dog's bellow Lothar checked in mid-stride. The dreaded dog scent smote him in the nostrils as he did so. He swung to the right, hesitated. Short on experience but long on fighting instinct, Wolf-Eye checked, also. The two fell into the circling tactic of the wolf. The she-wolf crouched, trembling.

The gladiators moved around the mountain arena. Underfoot the piñon-needle carpet deadened all sound. Overhead the moon gave good light.

Wolf-Eye lifted and reset each foot as though life depended on it—as, indeed, it did. One small misstep with an opponent like Lothar could be crucial. Lacking a battle plan, the dog passed the initiative to the wolf—waited for Lothar to make the first move.

The wolf sensed this reticence, and it made him overconfident, a fact that represented Wolf-Eye's sole asset in the beginning of the fight. Otherwise the power lay with the grizzled wolf, for, in the full of his ninth season, Lothar was a grim fighting machine. Every sure movement shouted— "Beware . . . danger!"—and his attitude of deliberation was enough to unnerve any adversary.

Across from him, equally impressive, padded the watchful Wolf-Eye. Taller than the wolf, heavier by thirty pounds, bigger-boned, younger, the strange-eyed shepherd was not a reassuring picture to his opponent. Heavy jaw muscles overlay his high-boned cheeks. His lips, writhing back till the gums were bared, revealing a perfect set of fighting teeth. His movements were crisp, light, and fast. His body was hard from months of work and training.

In physical equipment the dog was equal to the wolf. But in fighting skill? Experience? Ferocity? There the advantage lay heavily with Lothar.

Suddenly the wolf stopped circling. Across from him Wolf-Eye froze. Inch by inch Lothar crept across the circle. Wolf-Eye waited for him, crouching, ready.

There had been no sound in the arena for many seconds while the two circled. Now, with a deep snarl, Lothar charged. The unexpectedness of the sound unnerved Wolf-Eye. For a tenth of a second he hesitated. In that time Lothar's body had hurtled through fifteen feet of air and crashed shoulder to shoulder into him. Wolf-Eye was driven back on his haunches. A moment later he tumbled over onto his back. Lothar snarled triumphantly. A quick dive onto the prostrate dog, a ripping slash at the exposed throat, and all would be over. But instinct temporarily stayed the execution. Cat-like, Wolf-Eye bunched his feet the moment his back hit the ground. Thus Lothar's leap for the throat landed him, instead, on the dog's tucked-up feet. Wolf-Eye's hindquarters straightened with a snap. Lothar flew backward, to land on his own hindquarters. An experienced fighter would have been upon the wolf before he could recover, but Wolf-Eye merely gained his own feet and crouched to await Lothar's next move.

Puzzled, the old wolf hesitated. Then he returned to the attack. This time he came quartering in from a side angle— from the right side and apparently aiming at a point just behind the dog's shoulder. This ruse made the youngster expose his throat in turning to protect his shoulder. One step to the right shifted Lothar in mid-charge and without pause. Straight in for the throat he shot, whereas a moment before he had aimed for the shoulder.

Complete lack of skill saved Wolf-Eye. An old fighter would have turned just far enough to put his head in position for a slash at Lothar's head as the latter came in at the shoulder. Wolf-Eye turned too far—so far, in fact, that he brought his far shoulder clear around to the near, or attack, side. It was a clumsy, amateurish turn—and it saved his life. Lothar's surprised fangs ground into tough shoulder bone instead of soft throat tissue. The wolf's momentum carried him beyond and free of the dog.

For the second time Wolf-Eye had an opening. And for the second time he waited. Lothar had made two bad blunders; either would have cost him his life against experienced opponents. The dog had made no use of either chance. Lothar grunted. With a roar of disdainful anger he charged. In front of him the dog crouched, waiting. Lothar bore down in reckless frontal attack. The dog arose to meet him.

In mid-air their bodies met. Shoulder to shoulder they stood and fought. Fangs slashing, ears flattened, bodies straining, they twisted and struggled. Down they went, closely locked—over and over upon the ground. This was to the death.

The wolf fought with rasping snarls coming in continuous streams from his deep throat. The dog was silent.

Shortly after Lothar knew he had made a mistake in closing with the dog. He had deliberately thrown away his main advantage and brought the battle to the only place where his experience counted for nothing.

In the first head-on clash Wolf-Eye had borne Lothar to

earth, and, as the two rolled and thrashed around the floor of the clearing, the dog punished the wolf unmercifully. Lothar was beneath Wolf-Eye, with the latter trying for his throat. The best part of a decade of prairie warfare now came to the wolf's rescue.

Suddenly Lothar stiffened, relaxed, and lay still. Wolf-Eye paused. Lothar struck. Upward from the ground his head snaked toward the throat of the dog above him. Missing the throat (a deathblow from Lothar's position had been an outside chance), the wolf's fangs buried themselves in Wolf-Eye's breast. The reflex of pain forced the dog back, and Lothar was free.

Now, for a moment, the wolf would have paused, but not so the dog. Both combatants were badly wounded, but the pain of Lothar's fangs in his chest was too much for Wolf-Eye. Recklessly he charged the old wolf.

Here was what Lothar wanted—his opponent hot with rage, charging blindly from the front. It was all that the battle-wise old wolf had been waiting for. Uttering a loud grunt of pain, he stumbled and fell as though from injury or weakness. Triumphantly Wolf-Eye left his feet, rose in arching leap above the prostrate form of the old wolf. Instantly Lothar shot forward under the leaping dog.

At this point history disproved itself. Where the wolf sought to come in under the dog and disembowel him from a quick belly slash upward, he found no such soft target, for in his leap Wolf-Eye had turned and twisted in mid-air, thus throwing his unprotected belly to the side and presenting, instead, the bony toughness of a muscular haunch.

Nor was this all. As Lothar's fangs plowed into the muscles of Wolf-Eye's hindquarters, the dog was turning and coming downward upon Lothar's unguarded spine. There was a smashing impact as the dog's great weight came full upon the wolf's back, a splintering of bone blended with a horrible snarl from Lothar. Then there was silence save for the drip, drip of the blood from the gaping wound that was inches deep, a foot in length, a wound that stretched diagonally from the forepart of one shoulder to the elbow point of the opposite one—whose course plowed squarely across the spinal column in the region of the neck and shoulder juncture.

VII

"THE OUTLAW TRAIL"

With victory came the reaction. Wolf-Eye shook uncontrollably and felt a little sick. His wounds pained fiercely. He staggered a step forward. Nausea wracked him.

His left shoulder and right haunch were laid open to the bone, his head and neck marked with a dozen deep slashes. He looked uncertainly over toward the she-wolf. She whined softly for him to come to her. Gingerly he stepped over the dead body of Lothar. Slight as the movement was, it started his wounds afresh. His whole leg and side became dark and wet with the blood from his haunch. His eyes blurred, then cleared, and blurred again. The form of Vega receded and diminished to nothing. A rushing and roaring filled his head. A light airiness came to his feet. He stumbled twice before he fell.

Timed almost to the instant of his fall, the report of a rifle spat from the clearing's edge. The ugly *whang-eee* of the lead-nosed .30-30 slug whined over the dog's head. In the same moment the hemlocks at the far side of the clearing parted, and Jim Lewis ran swiftly forward.

But Vega, the she-wolf, was first to the dog's side. Frantically she tried to arouse her champion. With imperative shovings of her nose she urged him. Jim was very close now. With a parting snarl the she-wolf turned and disappeared. Jim stopped in surprise at the sight and sound of the female. He snapped a shell into the Winchester and fired, first from the hip, then two shoulder shots. But the wolf was gone.

Then the rancher discovered his bullet had not felled Wolf-Eye. In examining the dog his hand felt the haunch wound. It was pumping blood from a severed artery. He bent his ear to the dog's side. A relieved grin spread over his face. The big shepherd was still alive.

From the instant he had rushed out of the ranch house and found Wolf-Eye gone in response to the female's call, Jim had known that he could not persuade the shepherd away from the wolf. Therefore, he had taken the big dog's trail on the chance he might get a shot at him. With this shot Jim hoped to injure his dog just enough to allow him to recapture him. To hazard such a shot was to endanger the dog's life, but there was no other choice. If the dog were to stay with the wolf, he would thereby sign his own death warrant anyway. The risk of the crippling shot was Wolf-Eye's last, best chance of redemption from the outlaw trail onto which his pursuit of the red she-wolf would lead him. In the bad light of the moonlit clearing Jim had been afraid that this shot might be a killing one.

But, now, a swift tourniquet for the haunch and a cleansing of the less severe wounds and his dog stood a very good chance of survival. From the pack that Jim had made up at the ranch came creosote, sugar sacking, blanket pins, and a big roll of horse tape—crude adjuncts provided against the success of his first plan, the crippling shot. Quickly he worked, and with the deft skill of the veteran stockman.

Jim had good reason for the grim satisfaction that swelled within him. It was a lucky night for him and for his dog. Not only did he have Wolf-Eye back—which was enough—but the shepherd hadn't really gotten with the she-wolf, after all.

Wolf-Eye was still a man's dog. No mistake about that.

The warmth of the fire soon had Wolf-Eye coming around nicely. Seeing Jim, he essayed a shamefaced wag of his tail. This cost him a surprised grunt of pain. The rancher chuckled and smoothed his dog's head.

"Wolfie, you almost got yourself in trouble . . . real bad trouble," he said softly.

Wolf-Eye blinked, tried another painful tail wag. Then, licking his lips, he reached a stiff forepaw toward Jim. The man took the paw, and the dog's eyes closed wearily. In a short time he was sleeping.

"Me, too, boy," said Jim finally. "This night trailin' and mountain climbin' is not for your old boss."

Wolf-Eye whined and stirred in his sleep.

"We'll be home tomorrow, Wolfie," the rancher said.

Weary as he was, Jim took time to secure Wolf-Eye to a stout sapling with two lengths of horsehair lariat before turning in. The dog seemed quiet, but you could never tell. As an extra precaution he passed a length of the lariat around his own body. Then, at last satisfied, he lay down to sleep.

Wolf-Eye came awake. A growl rumbled in his chest and died at the same time. From the shadows stepped Vega, the she-wolf. With utter disdain she stepped over the sleeping Jim and came straight for Wolf-Eye. For an instant their noses met. Then the red female flicked out a sly tongue. Its caress lay lightly on the dog's muzzle. Before he could reply in kind, she had set to work on the ropes that held him. The tough horsehair was no match for her teeth. With rare judgment she cut the rope where it passed around Wolf-Eye's neck rather than from the tree or the sleeping human. Thus no appreciable movement took place, and Jim slept on.

Wolf-Eye tottered to his feet. Weak and shaky still, his

haunch suddenly pained him anew. The she-wolf nosed his wounds briefly; then, satisfied that he could travel, she turned to leave. As she did, her eyes fell upon Jim. She half crouched. The man was on his back, arms outstretched, throat bared. Ears flattening, Vega settled to spring.

But a shadow fell between her and her prey. She looked up to meet Wolf-Eye's cold stare. He regarded her unblinkingly. The she-wolf shivered. Some swift instinct struck a sudden fear to her wild heart, although she never knew how close she was to death at that moment. Unwittingly she had been about to transgress the one law in Wolf-Eye's life—Jim Lewis could not be harmed. She drew back, still under the spell of the dog's blazing eyes. He curled his lip over the ivory fangs beneath it. Vega turned and left the camp.

With one last look at his master Wolf-Eye followed her. Shoulder to shoulder the giant dog and the slim she-wolf made their way up the mountain. There was no pausing, no looking back.

Jim allowed himself the luxury of one yawning stretch, then sat up and blinked his eyes to adjust them to the brilliance of the morning sun. Turning to look at the injured shepherd, he started to call out cheerily.

"Hey, Wolfie. Get up, dog. We have to hike all the way back to. . . ." Jim broke off in mid-sentence, his face gray.

"Holy howlin' mavcricks." His voice was little more than a whisper. "He's gone! The big mutton-headed fool, why in the name of . . . ?" Again the rancher broke off his words as he eyes widened with amazement.

"It was that she-devil! Can you beat that?"

To a tracker like Jim the evidence was all too clear. A quick examination of the campsite confirmed his estimate. The wolf's tracks were clear as snow water.

Well, if that was the way the she-wolf wanted to play, good enough. And the same for Wolf-Eye. Jim could play rough, too.

The rancher's heart sank even as the thought formed. The dog's choice was beyond change now. If the chance came to Jim for another shot, it couldn't be a crippling one. The time for that was past. There would be no reclaiming of Wolf-Eye from the female now. They had taken the trail together.

Jim made up his pack and started off after the two fugitives. It was an easy trail, for the most part through snow and damp mountain earth. As he swung along the double line of tracks, Jim was thinking that he must get the female. He was almost positive he would come up with the pair before any mating took place, but the chance of wolf dog cubs being born in a stock country could not be gambled on. He must get the she-wolf.

Suddenly Jim dropped to one knee and studied a section of tracks closely. He grunted understandingly. With each print of the dog's right hind paw, there now appeared a bright crimson blotch. The rancher scooped up some of the reddened snow, sniffed at it, felt it carefully. It was fresh, even warm.

Higher yet Vega, the she-wolf, led Wolf-Eye, the shepherd dog. At first the traveling pair made fair time. But the steepening terrain soon opened Wolf-Eye's haunch wound, and the blotches on the trail became bigger and closer together. From time to time the dog staggered and would have fallen but for the ready support of the she-wolf's shoulder.

Shortly Vega made a halt. Leaving Wolf-Eye in the shelter of a granite outcropping, she backtracked to a point that gave a view of the last two or three miles of their progress. Topping a final rise in the back trail, she almost stepped on Jim Lewis.

He was crouching in the snow, examining the trail not three hundred feet away. He saw her as she dived back for cover, snapped two quick shots at her with the rifle cradled near his hip and without shifting his ground position—misses, of course. He could see the granite fly from the outcropping upon which the wolf stood.

He pumped a fresh cartridge into the Winchester. The she-wolf would have the dog close by. With a satisfied nod he took up the trail. There was no hurry, he knew. The amount of blood in the trail told him the dog was done for. If only the wolf would stay around him!

As Vega fled, a desperate thought formed in her mind. About three hundred yards beyond Wolf-Eye's hiding place the trail narrowed to an inches-wide ledge, several hundred feet in length. She knew the spot well. Many times she had found it useful, and now she would put it to the real test.

Halfway along its snow-clad length was an overhanging precipice of rotten ice formed by the winter-frozen fall of a small stream above. Here one must go very carefully, for the slightest jarring misstep might set up a vibration that could loosen the thousands of tons of delicately poised rock and snow above, sending half the mountainside plunging down. Below the trail at this point was a drop of several hundred feet, sloping to a forty-five-degree pitch, that continued downward through the timberline and into the forest below, a distance of three or four thousand feet in all. It was a descent at which the bravest heart might hesitate. But Vega was determined to try it. The death it might bring would be preferable by far to that from the searing rupture of a rifle bullet.

Between Wolf-Eye and the beginning of the glacial ledge lay a quarter-mile meadow of open snow. Somehow the injured dog must be gotten across this before Lewis approached. Vega called to Wolf-Eye in a high, warning yelp.

He got to his feet and swung unsteadily in beside her. Together they raced across the meadow. Halfway across, the
dog faltered, but the she-wolf drove her teeth into his rump,
and he shot forward with a grunt of pained surprise. As they
turned the ledge, a shower of flying ice spattered about their
haunches. There came to them, on the heels of this, the dry
spat of a rifle. Lewis was in the meadow.

Under the she-wolf's urging, Wolf-Eye managed to reach
the rotten ice, but there he slumped down. At that moment
Jim rounded the ledge and opened fire. His first shot tore a
jagged wound in Vega's side, but before he could correct his
range, the she-wolf began an action that stopped his rifle
halfway to his shoulder.

Leaping over Wolf-Eye, where he lay on the last of the
solid ice, she ran out onto the thin ledge of rotten ice beyond.
There she began to leap into the air and come down with her
legs stiff, in a series of short jumps. At the fourth or fifth jump
she turned in mid-air and leaped back to Wolf-Eye and the
solid portion of the ledge. As she landed, the mountain above
seemed to burst forth and belch out its heart.

Jim watched, unbelieving, as a section of the mountain
came away from its place above the trail and, crashing downward, swept away the trail and continued on down the precipice. Columns of snow dust filled the air for hundreds of feet,
and for many seconds the rancher could see nothing. Then,
as the air cleared, he could make out the she-wolf huddled
over the inert form of Wolf-Eye on what remained of the
ledge. A dozen feet beyond the two there was no ledge, and
the dying trail of the avalanche thundered past. Below them
the fallen mass of ice and snow had piled up upon itself and
obliterated the vertical drop, assuming the forty-five-degree
angle of the slope below. Now, from the ledge to the timber
below, there stretched an unbroken snow slide. Even as the

last tons of snow were moving down from above, and while the whole surface of the slide was still in motion, Vega seized Wolf-Eye by the scruff of the neck and, with a powerful lunge, propelled both the dog and herself off the end of the broken ledge and onto the rumbling bosom of the slide.

Jim watched the two tiny figures negotiate the entire length of the slide. Rolling, tumbling, bouncing head over heels, they were soon lost in the spume of snow at the slide's end. Whether the she-wolf and his dog lay safely in the forest below or were crushed beneath tons of rock and ice, Jim found it impossible to surmise. He studied the spot through his binoculars.

After several seconds he mused to himself. *That's the spot, all right . . . about three or four hundred yards from where the ledge begins. That slide is nearly a mile long, reaches clear down to the timber. Man alive! There's just a chance she got away with it. Guess it's up to me to find out anyway. Got to, I reckon.*

The day was well spent, but he figured he could get to the bottom of the slide before nightfall. However, darkness caught him still some way from the spot he had marked through the glasses for the beginning of his search. The broken mass poured down by the avalanche did not present the kind of terrain a wise man undertook in bad light, so he decided to save it for daylight. He made his camp near the edge of the slide, and the rich smell of broiling bacon was soon vying with the pine and snow scents. Before long, supper finished, Jim was fast asleep.

VIII
"WILD VICTORY"

Amid the roar of the avalanche Vega and Wolf-Eye careened down the mountainside. Great boulders and huge blocks of snow revolved over and about them. Time and again Vega felt bone-wrenching shocks as she collided with some whirling piece of débris. She clung fiercely to Wolf-Eye, constantly tightening her jaws on the dog's heavy ruff. Finally she suffered one blinding smash and lost consciousness.

As her wind returned, Vega's first thought was for her mate. Struggling to regain her feet, she found that, strain as she might, she could not move. She was trapped, jammed tightly up against a tree trunk beneath the surface of the slide. Above her she could see a patch of sky. She could feel no movement in the walls of her prison and judged the avalanche had come to rest.

She lay dozing in her ice-lined tomb, and soon she became aware of a distant scratching. Her vision was clouded, and objects would not assume definite outlines. She felt, rather than saw, a blurred movement taking place about the opening above. Vague sounds came to her. Then all sound faded. For an instant she saw two great yellow eyes peering down upon her. They receded swiftly—burned quickly out. For the second time that day the she-wolf lost consciousness.

Hours went by before the blackness lifted. Night came

before the green eyes of the she-wolf opened again. At first, there was no sound about her, just a grateful warmth and quiet. Then she became aware of heavy breathing and of a great weight bearing down upon her flanks. Frightened, she turned her head. Stretched across her, eyes closed, head buried in the piñon needles, breath coming in sobbing gasps, was Wolf-Eye.

The she-wolf found her feet and stood, looking at her chosen one in terror. Somehow this young gray giant must be made to live. She must find a way to do this. The dog must have labored untold hours to release her from her frozen cell. How he had managed to get her out of her prison was a mystery, but what she, Vega, must do in return was no mystery. She must find food and bring it to him. She had to do that or he would die.

Wildly the young she-wolf fled the cedar tangle where Wolf-Eye had brought her. She had not taken a dozen steps before she froze in her tracks and flattened in the snow. A hundred paces upwind a human figure lay by the smoldering embers of a small fire. The odor of broiled meat hung in the night air. The she-wolf's nostrils trembled; her jaws began to champ nervously. Suddenly she went forward through the snow, circling the flickering fire and bearing down on the rear of the slumbering figure by its side.

For the second time within twenty-four hours Vega invaded the camp of a hated human. For the second time she worked within inches of the man, in spite of the devastating fear she felt for his species. Immediately she began to nose about for the origin of the meat smell that had lured her. An almost noiseless growl escaped her throat. The delicious meat was in the man's pack—and the man was using his pack for a pillow!

Gingerly the she-wolf took hold of one of the pack straps. She tugged. It moved a little, then locked against the man's arm. She tried her teeth on the pack cover. The first contact of her teeth with the stiff canvas brought forth a harsh, grating noise. Alarmed, Vega sprang back and crouched, her eyes riveted on the sleeping man. He only stirred a little, then relaxed.

She set to work, her mind made up to try the hazardous job of tugging the pack out from under the man's head. Laying hold of the free end of one of the straps, she pulled gently. In three minutes of cautious work she had moved the pack an inch. In five minutes she had moved it three inches. In ten, almost a foot. She shook violently; saliva poured from her trembling jaws. A second more and the job was done.

With the pack free it was the work of only an instant for the she-wolf to grab it in her jaws, clear the dying fire with a cat-like leap, and race back to Wolf-Eye's side.

Seizing the chunk of raw bacon, she forced one end of it under the dog's nose. He turned his head weakly and started to close his eyes. With a savage growl Vega again shoved the meat under his nose. Again she growled. Apathetically the big dog opened his jaws. Vega forced the meat between them. Wolf-Eye tried to chew, but could not. Instead, he dropped the meat and fell to licking it. Vega allowed him to continue this for several minutes, encouraging him with low growls. Then she once more forced the chunk between his unwilling jaws. This time he made a fair attempt at gnawing one corner of the piece. The she-wolf helped him at once, tearing the meat in shreds and offering him the small pieces one at a time. He began to eat, at first only the shreds of lean, then larger chunks of the pure fat.

When Jim awoke, his first sensation was that of an unaccountably stiff neck. Reaching to adjust the pack, he was suddenly awake. The pack was gone. A quick examination of the campsite revealed a maze of wolf tracks.

"That beats me," breathed the rancher. "Do you suppose that . . . ? No, that couldn't be! Whoever this cuss was, he must sure enough have been starvin' to death to come into a man's camp so boldly."

For an instant Jim thought again of the audacious red female, then put the idea from him. It just didn't make sense.

Nevertheless the man was determined to run the tracks out if he could. Starting at the fire, he worked a widening circle around it. On the third circle, about a hundred yards from the fire and close to a dense cedar and piñon tangle, he caught fresh wolf sign. The track led directly into the tangle. Inside he found a jumble of tracks and the remains of his pack. A clot or two of blood on the torn canvas cover interested him, and he stooped to make a closer examination. Jim whistled softly. What a nervy rascal! The sign couldn't have been more than ten minutes old. On the underside of a low-hanging cedar limb, adhering to the rough bark by a small clot of drying blood, was a tuft of reddish-gold hair. Incredible. It *had* been that red she-devil who robbed him, after all.

Seeking for the wolf's point of exit from the thicket, he stumbled on a line of wolf tracks that led straight out across the snows of the avalanche. But it was not these that caused his mouth to go wide in amazement.

"Wolf-Eye, by heaven!" he gasped.

Side by side with the she-wolf's long, narrow tracks stretched the huge, broad footprints of the giant shepherd.

"Son-of-a-gun," breathed Jim. "A hundred yards more and I'd have stumbled right over him. What a break! A few more steps last night and I would have had him!"

Fortunately for Vega and Wolf-Eye, Jim was now forced to

return to his campsite and make up his pack before taking their trail. The she-wolf made good use of the extra time, and, when Jim headed out across the rough snowfield of the avalanche, she had gotten the wounded dog miles away.

For two days the rancher kept up the pursuit. Then the fading trail headed for lower ground where sharp-banked dry washes crisscrossed every mile of the way. As if to supply the closing argument for Jim's decision to abandon the chase, the trail veered out of the hill country and across the trackless mesa.

"That's just about that," mumbled the weary hunter. "I'm not lookin' for any wolf-needle in that sandy haystack."

For a little while, then, he stood looking out into the emptiness of the flat country. Finally the bitterness faded from his face.

"Well, anyway, Wolfie," he chuckled, "you picked a smart gal for yourself. You sure as everlastin' thunder did."

IX

"FATHERHOOD"

Wolf-Eye was saddled with a problem of compound interest. Ordinarily a she-wolf, about to have pups, worries only about a safe place within which to shelter her brood, secure in the knowledge that the wolf is an able provider. But Vega was faced with the doubtful quantity of Wolf-Eye's skill in the chase. For all his great strength, the dog was still a clumsy hunter. Vega had done what she could to show her mate the principles of the stalk and the kill. The dog was an apt pupil, but the skills obtaining to a lifetime of wilderness training are not to be acquired overnight.

He had her help as he approached the problem of providing food for his coming family. Vega sought to den up in the richest game region available, a ten-mile stretch of the eastern slope of Wildcat Mountain, heavily timbered and watered and well sprinkled with the thick grass meadows and birch and alder brakes so dear to the hoofed and antlered tribe. In a normal mating the she-wolf's choice of a den would have been one high above the timberline in that arid vastness of crags and monoliths where the track scent dies quickly on the naked rock and an enemy may be seen five miles ahead of his smell.

It was risky denning in the lower timber, with its scent-hoarding carpet of leaf and needle mold, its view-killing

61

stands of pine and tangled scrub, its uncomfortable closeness to the haunts of man and his wandering livestock. But the birth warnings were upon the red she-wolf, and her time was only hours distant.

Whimpering and grunting, she led Wolf-Eye deeper into the country of her selection. Her breathing was labored, for the way was steep and tortuous, but the mind of the young she-wolf was filled with the thought of finding a den. That Wolf-Eye's sons and daughters might be born in safety was her whole concern now. Wolf-Eye kept at her flank in anxious guard, nuzzling encouragement where the trail steepened, lending a muscular shoulder for assistance where the going roughened.

Presently the course of the brawling stream they were following was bisected by a brush-choked dry wash whose floor level overhung that of the streambed. Into this Vega scrambled and with sudden eagerness began following its twisted upward path. Shortly the grade leveled and the wash widened, while the sheltered side walls grew higher and more precipitous. Vega paused. Here lay what she sought—a perfect wilderness nursery. She let her tired eyes dwell on each welcome detail. The clearing was roughly circular, with red clay walls a dozen feet high and so near the perpendicular as to appear overhanging. Around the edges were heaped piles of small boulders, while in one corner, wedged tightly in a jam of rock, lay the uprooted butt of a four-foot cedar. The same flood that had brought the cedar stump down had scooped out the bank behind it, creating an ideal and natural retreat. So small was the opening to this hideaway that the heavy she-wolf could scarcely force her weary bulk through it.

Once inside the entrance, she paused to let her eyes absorb the heavy dark. In a moment she saw before her the end of her journey. The cavern was small, yet ample for the purpose. In height it cleared a tall wolf's shoulder. In width it was two body lengths and in length, four. The floor was level, dry sand. In one corner was a drift of soft pine needles. Upon this bed Vega turned twice around and lay down with a deep grunt.

The she-wolf relaxed. Here in the den it was dry and warm. Outside she could see the outline of her mate's shoulder where he lay at guard by the entrance. As she watched, he raised his head and swung his nostrils back and forth across the night wind. Then, appearing satisfied, he lowered it again. Turning to the cave, he uttered a growl of assurance. All was well. Vega whimpered softly in reply.

Sometime later that night Wolf-Eye was awakened by sounds issuing from within the den—thin little yips and wailings that threw every hair on his spine erect. He leaped to his feet and promptly cracked his head on an overhanging root. The blow loosened a shower of rotten granite that fell into his eyes and set him to pawing his face. Shortly he remembered the original cause of his alarm. Thrusting his head into the den, he nearly got his nose snapped off. Later he was to know that no wilderness mother allows the father near the young at first, but now he was hurt by Vega's reception.

After his rebuff he sat for a while outside the cave, pondering his mate's behavior. Presently the whimperings inside the den grew louder, and he could no longer restrain his curiosity.

Edging closer to the cave mouth, he tried another glance within. Once more he was met by Vega's scolding snarls. And once more he withdrew in haste. As his confusion mounted and self-pity hunched his shoulders, he took pause to note that the whimperings within the cave had been replaced by comparative quiet. At once his worrying gave way to that imperative curiosity that is the instinct of all young fathers.

He raised his head hopefully. What kind of sound was that? A tiny grunting and gurgling and much-satisfied smacking of small lips. Very interesting. If Vega weren't in such a foul temper, one might look in there and see for himself what went on.

Wolf-Eye fidgeted, made obvious noises, yawned, stretched, sighed. No result. He whined questioningly. Still no response from Vega. Finally he growled demandingly. At this the she-wolf took note and growled back at him. Wolf-Eye, thinking he detected a note of softness in the growl, went at once to the cave entrance. Vega growled again, giving him apparent permission to come in. This he did, but at first, since his eyes were not yet used to the pitch black of the interior, he saw nothing. Then the hair went up on his back, and he withdrew a step, startled.

There they were, nursing and squirming at Vega's breasts like so many furry little rats. Wolf-Eye couldn't get out of that cave fast enough. Now he really was confused.

Outside, he worked his way down the wash to the streambed. Here he paused to collect himself. He had been in many jams before this, and dangerous ones, too. There had been the killing of the huge Brahma steer, and that of old Lothar, the wolf, and the matter of the maddened mother cow at the calf roundup. But they had involved nothing more precious than his own thick-furred neck.

Now he had eight necks to preserve, without once thinking of his own. He tried to remember what those children of his looked like. Horrible-looking they were, he decided, stepping cautiously out on the first stone of the stream crossing. There was also a tremendous lightness in Wolf-Eye's bosom. The young dog could not know it, but the pride of fatherhood was upon him. The more he grumbled about the unpleasantness of his new family, the lighter his tread became. The greater his sorrow with parenthood, the higher the tilt of his head. Soon, with increasing realization of his position, he was nearly bursting with pride. And long before he reached the other side of the stream, his mounting ego led to the careful placing of a forepaw squarely upon a rock that wasn't there. *Splash! Krrumph!* Wolf-Eye was down by the stern in four feet of roaring mountain water. Thirty feet downstream he was cast up, head and paws together, on a shelving sandbar.

He landed with enough force to drive the wind out of him, but he got up and splashed ashore as though nothing had happened. Starting off through the woods, he bumped and banged into trees; snapped through dry bushes; stepped on loudly popping twigs; and, in general, violated every rule of good hunting.

Soon a wayward rabbit, fascinated by the carelessness of Wolf-Eye's approach, bobbed up across his trail. Wolf-Eye made chase and killed mechanically. Just as thoughtlessly he set to the feast. It was only after the third bite that he thought of Vega. She would like some of this juicy young rabbit. He must remember to leave a little to take home to her. She was particularly partial to young rabbit. He broke off the feast and swung his great head up with an amazed look in his wide, yellow eyes. He had forgotten the family! This would never do.

In a moment he was all anxiety. Already the east showed pale over the piñon grove to his right. Not more than an hour's good hunting was left. The situation was no longer an idle one. If he missed his kill tonight, it might be twenty-four hours before he could make another.

From wandering new father to concentrating killer, the transformation was swift and complete. Hurriedly Wolf-Eye circled the wind until it blew fresh and clean in his face. Eagerly he quartered, working over deeper into the thickening copses of birch and alder.

Luck was with him. Not more than twenty minutes had passed before the dawn wind gave news of game ahead. A few feet farther on he cut a deeply rutted deer trail. Quickly he lowered his head. The deer tracks seemed to leap at him from the soft loam of the forest floor. They were not minutes old. The loam still moved, a piece of it toppling from a track edge even as Wolf-Eye watched. Elated, he advanced along the animal's trail at a near gallop.

The deer, a fat two-year-old buck, was traveling leisurely across an open meadow when Wolf-Eye came up to him. He was just beginning to browse. Lazily he pawed in the fresh snow for grasses or nipped at a stray twig or tender young shag of birch bark.

The shepherd watched him coldly, carefully computed the time it would take him to graze across the open to the far side of the meadow, weighed this against the time it would take him, Wolf-Eye, to circle the meadow and prepare an ambush. The gamble looked good.

When the dog drew into his chosen spot on the far side of the clearing, he was not quite prepared for the precision of his calculations. The big buck was fifteen feet from his cover and moving directly toward it. He had finished grazing and was walking with purposeful steps toward the forest's edge. He would pass within five feet of Wolf-Eye. The shepherd had scarcely time to gather his hindquarters under him before the moment of attack came.

Like a thick-furred thunderbolt he smashed shoulder to shoulder into the young buck. Surprise and brute force carried the attack. The buck's forefeet were smashed out from under him, and he went down in front as though shot through the brain. Before he could move to recover, the great dog's jaws sheared through the spinal vertebrae just behind the head.

Wolf-Eye stepped back from his kill. He felt fresh and good and strong. It had been easy. Vega would have liked the professional way he had done it. She would have been proud. His children would have been proud. As a matter of fact, he was proud.

As he worked to get a chosen hindquarter free of the carcass, he noted that a storm was blowing up. The temperature was dropping rapidly. Wolf-Eye growled apprehensively and fell to his butchering with redoubled intentness. Soon he had the quarter free and, seizing the great chunk of meat in his jaws, started on the back trail. In spite of his strength the weight of the prize bore his head downward. Before he had gone half a mile, he was near exhaustion. Obviously here was a time for invention. Another few minutes would so exhaust his jaw muscles that they would be unable to hold the weight of the meat, let alone transport it.

Despair came over him. With a roar he threw himself on the quarter and, seizing it by a thick stringer of flesh, began shaking it savagely. Presently the fit of anger passed, and he stood quivering in the shame of his weakness. As he stood, he noticed that the meat, although still in his jaws, had lost its drugging weight. Surprised, he turned his head—thinking to see the main chunk lying in the trail, since it must have come loose from the part he still held in his mouth. He was further surprised to find that this was not the case and that, as a matter of fact, the big quarter, still attached firmly to the trailing piece he held in his mouth, was resting comfortably across his broad shoulders.

He took a few steps. The meat jolted around but remained firmly in place. There was no strain on his jaws. Already the strength was flowing back into them. Wolf-Eye broke into a trot. A mile fell away. The question of transport was wondrously solved.

If a dog can grin, especially with a haunch of venison in his jaws, Wolf-Eye grinned then. What matter that accident had stepped in where judgment had failed?

An hour later, full-fed and happy, he drowsed in the warmth of the cave. Outside, the force of a high country blizzard yammered and threatened. Vega grunted and sighed blissfully. Wolf-Eye stole a sleepy glance at her, then composed himself for slumber.

In all the world there was nothing but peace for Wolf-Eye.

X
"WOLF-EYE BURIES THE PAST"

Came a night, though, before long, when peace fled forever from Wolf-Eye. All during his courtship of the red she-wolf, the big shepherd dog had been unable to erase Jim from his thoughts. To eyes and ears and nose as keen as Wolf-Eye's, the range was strewn with signs and reminders of his master. At the ashes of a calf-branding fire, there would be a certain twisted piece of half-smoked cigarette. There would be other cigarettes; but this one would bear the sign of Jim's fingers, and the magic nose of Wolf-Eye would tell him this. There would be a partic-ular line of horse tracks, and Wolf-Eye would know that, among the dozens of other lines of horse tracks, this line was laid down by a mount that had borne Jim Lewis on its back. There would be a lone shred of faded blue denim clinging to a sharp claw of tall-growing cactus, and this, to Wolf-Eye, would read Jim Lewis as clearly as any painted signpost.

So it was that the dog was unable to forget the man. But with the advent of the pups he became so busy hunting and foraging for their food and so intrigued with the manner and rapidity of their growth that, in truth, he did forget Jim. These were the only completely happy weeks the big dog had known since leaving Wolf Creek Ranch.

By day he would roll and play with the fat little cubs for hours on end, never seeming to tire of their sprawling antics.

He was absorbed by them and found in them much of the pleasure and playfulness he had missed in his own puppyhood.

By night, however, the great gray dog became the silent ranger of the forest and grassland slopes. With the death of the sun and the birth of the moon, he slipped as easily from the rôle of fond father to that of cold-blooded hunter as one might change a pair of shoes. Those few weeks with the puppies provided Wolf-Eye with his first relief from the gnawing hunger he had felt for the hand and sound and smell of Jim Lewis. This relief, however, was to be short-lived and, once gone, was never to return again.

One night Wolf-Eye was running his usual hunt in the excellent game country among the piñon-studded slopes above Portal Rocks. The big shepherd had had no particular luck and was about to work his way down to the lower grasslands when the sudden sting of woodsmoke smote his nostrils. Hard on the smoke odor came another even more pungent one. It was the man smell of Jim Lewis—deep, impelling, close by.

The dog dropped to his belly among the tall, dry grasses. Silently as the smoke itself, he went forward to the man smell. In a moment his slanted golden eyes were peering through a screen of cedar scrub. The deep red of shifting firelight splashed at the surrounding black of the cedar grove. Unwinking, the shepherd's strange yellow eyes followed the movements of the tall man squatted by the fire's side.

Since losing Wolf-Eye to Vega in the aftermath of the snow slide, Jim had abandoned the hunt, but he had not forgotten that the code of the stockman foreswore him ever really to do so. He realized that the result of his dog's disaffection would be a litter of half-wolf pups and that these cubs not only would be raised in the wolf tradition but would have, as well, all the advantages of the dog's training in the ways of man. Such a litter presented far greater danger to the range-land stock than would a pure wolf litter. The annals of all stock countries are replete with records of renegade, half-dog killers.

Thus Jim, while not devoting his full time to the problem of bringing Wolf-Eye in, still managed to plan his trips around the range so that they would take in those parts of the land that he considered Wolf-Eye's most likely choice of hunting and living quarters. It was significant that his un-varying companion on these trips was the Winchester saddle gun, snug in its underknee scabbard.

The Wolf Creek rancher had a code of his own in this search. If he were to have a chance at the dog, he would take it. He would never let a full, fair shot go by. If he could be the agent of a clean, painless end for the gray dog, he would not hesitate. At the same time, he would use no least advantage that his man's mind gave him over the dog he loved so well. He would not, for instance, call or whistle through the wilder-ness for Wolf-Eye. He would not in any way lure the dog to him by using the dog's love for him. The rancher knew it was his duty to destroy the dog, and he would not, when the time came, shrink from this duty. By the same token, he would never betray him. In this way, then, and under these terms did the rancher come to be, on a certain night in mid-March, encamped in the cedar timber above Portal Rocks.

Ten feet from the thing he loved more than all else in life, Wolf-Eye crouched in silence. Those ten feet might as well have been ten times as many miles. Across those few steps the young shepherd dog knew he could never go again. While life was in him, he could never know the touch of that hand or the sound of that voice speaking his name.

Who can say what force told Wolf-Eye these things? Why didn't the young dog bound out of hiding and frolic down upon his master? Why did he cower in the shadows like any wolf, when all he need do was romp forth and act as he always before had acted with Jim? Had Wolf-Eye changed? Did he no longer love the man by the fire? The pain and longing in his deep chest were intense. At that moment he would instantly have chosen to die, if by so doing he could first have heard his master's voice in softness, felt his hand in caress.

But a force stronger than all the dog-love in the world held Wolf-Eye as firmly in place as though he were bound there by chains of steel. It was a force older by countless centuries than either Jim or the shepherd dog. It was the force of faith—the treaty of faith, signed by the first hairy cave man with the first skulking wolf dog. It was this treaty and this faith that Wolf-Eye had broken. He was now cast out, forever, from among the faithful. Search as he might, Jim would never find his dog now. What he would find would not be a dog, but a beast. A wild thing of the wastelands. An outlaw. A wolf.

Hour upon hour passed, and the embers of Jim's fire faded into nothingness. Long since, the man's regular breathing in sleep had possessed the woodland silences. Deep night drew to morning stars, and morning stars to graying dawn—and only then did the watching yellow eyes forsake their lonely vigil. Before they disappeared, their owner stole forth like a great gray wraith and came to the side of the sleeping man. For long minutes he laid there, his nostrils breathing in the deep heart's ease of Jim's personal scent. Every minute variation in this man smell was restored carefully to his memory. Every last trace of it was distilled and filed away for future dreams. Saddle leather, dusty denim, Bull Durham, cow and horse smell—and, above all, the clean fresh smell that was the man's own. Mixed with the dawn fragrance of pine and cedar and dew-filled mountain grass and you have the memory of Jim Lewis that Wolf-Eye bore away with him, for a dog remembers with his nose, which is different from a mind—because a nose cannot forget.

One other thing Wolf-Eye bore away with him besides the memory. It was a glove, one of Jim's old, hard-worn, riding gloves. A thing of leather and sweat and stain it was—an old useless thing, without value.

Far up onto the outermost crest of the mightier of the Portal Rocks, Wolf-Eye bore the glove. There he carefully placed it in a secret cranny, an unknown crevice in the ageless tower, and covered it over with chips of rotten stone and the scalings of decomposing granite. Then, having buried it, he lay down beside it with his head stretched toward it and his body motionless. And so he remained, all through that day and until far past the appearance of the moon the following night.

XI

"STARVATION STRIKES"

The pups, now six weeks old, were fully weaned, and Vega, her old slim self, was able to join Wolf-Eye in the hunting. Even so, it was a task to feed the litter. Somehow they managed. Wolf-Eye had grown skillful and deadly in his style, and Vega, of course, was a past mistress. Between them, and what with hunting twenty-hour shifts and sleeping four, they kept the pups fed. They themselves might grow gaunt and vacant-eyed, but their family, in the midst of the worst hunting winter of a decade, grew fat and strong and straight-limbed.

Of the seven whelps, six were sons and the seventh a dainty daughter. The appearance of the six male cubs was peculiar but faithful to the mating that produced it. They were black-masked like Wolf-Eye. Also they had their sire's jet-black back-saddle and the black-arrow tail markings of the shepherd breed. Their dam's red body color, unusual in the wolf, stained every hair of their bodies not already claimed by their sire's gleaming black. The ears were small, the eyes of an unwinking gray-yellow so like that from which their sire had drawn his name. And yet there was a difference—the eyes of Wolf-Eye's sons were shallow and shifting, whereas the dog's were deep and steady.

The skulls of the cubs were flat and without apparent stop at the eyes. The muzzles broad and powerful, the jaws lumped with muscle together with the slit-mouths running far back under the ears, completed the picture of wolf heritage. Add the high-withered, lean-hipped angulation of the wolf tribe, the splayed feet and the resultant slouching gait, and the canvas of heredity had its final color. Physically they were, in small part, Wolf-Eye. Mentally they were all Vega.

The six sons were named Akhab, Barek, Korok, Sonjii, Rakar, and Bulop. These were wolf names and meant little to Wolf-Eye. To Vega each had its significance. Akhab meant the Brave. Barek, the Strong. Korok, the Crafty. Sonjii, the Wise. And Rakar, the Cruel. The other male, Bulop, was literally called Lop Ear for the comic manner in which his left ear, crippled at the base at birth, overhung his eye.

The lone daughter's name was Bini. In the wolf tongue Bini is the name for anything soft. Vega had given the name to her daughter with the faintest trace of derision. In the wolf code Bini is not a complimentary name. But Wolf-Eye was not yet subject to the wolf code, and he worshiped his daughter. Almost from the first she adopted her father's heels as the most pleasant place on earth around which to spend her time. And Wolf-Eye, for the most part, was more than pleased with the arrangement.

In appearance the she-cub was much like Vega. She had her mother's red coat and slim figure. But she was without the she-wolf's wild beauty and fascinating savagery of expression.

As the weeks fled springward, the big shepherd's relations with his little wolf-daughter became swiftly stronger. Vega and the six sons hunted frequently together, while Bini learned and grew under her sire. From him she received her first training in the hunt, the avoidance of traps and poison, and in the fundamentals of the simple canine tongue. Thus the companionship of Wolf-Eye and his daughter grew into a thing of constancy.

The interval between suns shortened; the snow withdrew from the Mogollons and retreated to the upper ranges of old Wildcat. Tiny new grasses and pygmy wild flowers sprang up overnight. The whole region re-clothed for spring. Life picked up tempo among the animals. Those who were of the grass-eaters fattened upon the new forage; those who were not of the grass-eaters fattened by less pleasant means.

It was a time to renew strength, and the gaunt Wolf-Eye clan hurried to fill its ravenous maw with the vernal crop of young cottontails, prairie dogs, marmots, ground squirrels, and the like. So bounteous was the rabbit supply that only the wisest of the meat hunters noticed the unusual scarcity of deer. The rains had hardly begun when the dry heat of summer came, two moons early. Snarling uneasily, the she-wolf concluded that the mesa would be dead beneath the unusual heat within one more moon.

Vega's fears were borne out. An occasional thin, tough old buck was encountered, but by August there was simply not enough food available. On top of that the blazing heat made daytime hunting impossible, limiting what foraging there was to the night hours. The pups grew gaunt and hollow-eyed and whined continuously among themselves.

Vega's hour of decision came. She knew that at any time, and without warning, starvation might reach the point where weakness would make further hunting impossible. She could not sit helplessly and watch her children die. Her mother's fierce love would not let her do it. Her mind closed like a steel trap once she had made her decision. There would be no altering of the course now. The choice was forced. They would kill the cattle.

With low whines the she-wolf called the cubs about her and, when they had come, uttered the fierce growl that always announced the beginning of the hunt. Hearing the hunting growl, Wolf-Eye came alert. The hunting-growl, given now when there was no game, could mean but one thing. His mate had decided to lead the cubs on a cattle kill. There could be no other explanation.

The sons began at once to snarl their approval. Wolf-Eye made no sound, only sat and stared cold-eyed into the gathering twilight. He, too, knew hunger. It had ridden him without mercy for unbroken weeks. Its every sign was emblazoned on him. His belly was pinched and shrunken to nothingness. His muscles sagged beneath folds of loose hide. His skin was a mass of open sores. The membranes of his mouth were raw with fever blisters. The tips of his ears, his muzzle, and the area around his eyes were inflamed from the attacks of the black and white deer flies. The eyes themselves were running mucus, and the nose was cracked and dry. The end was in sight, and Vega's decision was beyond challenge. Presently she came to him and with her were Akhab, Barek, Korok, Sonjii, Lop Ear, and Rakar. With deep snarls the she-wolf announced the hunt.

Wolf-Eye rumbled low in his chest. It was the waiting growl. When he had given it, he turned and faded into the darkness. Vega and the impatient cubs growled and snarled angrily—especially Rakar, the Cruel One. He knew where the dog had gone. They all knew. Bini, the she-cub, lay dying in the den. Their father had gone to moon over her, his favorite. Meanwhile, the cattle must wait.

Rakar, the impatient, the hotheaded, had had enough of this waiting. His growlings rose in excitement, but suddenly they broke off short, and a nervous silence fell among the group. Wolf-Eye's gaunt bulk loomed through the darkness. Like a shadow he came from the shadows to stand among them. The cubs shrank back instinctively, most of them seeking their mother's side. The flame-yellow eyes of the great shepherd burned as though with inner fires. If he had heard the rebellious snarlings of Rakar, he gave no sign. Only Rakar, of all the cubs, failed to draw back before the silent dog.

Without hesitation Wolf-Eye gave the hunting growl, and without hesitation Vega and the cubs started off. The she-wolf, surprised, stopped and looked back. Her great mate was not coming. He was standing back there by the den, his eyes boring through the night after them. She whined anxiously, but the big dog only repeated the hunting growl, and so she turned to lead the cubs away. Wolf-Eye would join them later, as was sometimes his habit.

The lights of Wolf Creek Ranch twinkled in the clear Arizona night. They beckoned to Wolf-Eye as he toiled over the three-mile breadth of Cedar Flats. He paused for a moment and looked ahead. Apparently satisfied, he continued on. Soon he broke from the concealing mesquite clusters of the Flats and stood, etched in the starlight, a scant quarter mile from the main ranch building.

Suspended from his powerful jaws hung a large, limp bundle of thin fur and bony paws—Bini, the she-cub. They had come a ten-mile journey, she and Wolf-Eye, and for the better part of it the great dog had carried her. Carefully the big shepherd laid the wasted form of the little female cub in the shelter of a low-growing juniper bush. Softly he uttered a growl of encouragement before padding forward into the darkness of the sheds and corrals.

Seemingly his master had not replaced him. This was satisfying. Silently he slipped past the last shed and slunk across the back yard. Head low, ears forward, feet stepping prettily as a cat's, he came beneath the open window of Jim's bedroom. Gathering his feet beneath him, he leaped to the thick adobe sill of the window. Here he crouched, half in, half out of the window, eyes peering into the darkness of the room.

His master was there. Eyes, ears, and nose brought the message simultaneously. A tremendous surge of homesickness seized Wolf-Eye. The sight and smell and sound of the man were almost more than he could bear. For one crazy instant the thought of not returning to Vega and the cubs came to him. But the remembrance of what had brought him here sobered him. He dropped to the ground and fled back through the gloom. When he returned again to the bedroom window, he was not alone.

Inside the room there was no sound as the huge dog eased himself to the floor. Gingerly he stepped across to the bed. With extreme care—care approaching reverence—he laid the unconscious she-cub at his master's feet. For a moment he stood looking down at her, then gave her a final tongue caress, and stepped cautiously back.

Jim had not stirred. Wolf-Eye regarded his master steadily. Stepping closer, he stretched his neck until his muzzle brushed the sleeping man's cheek. Unblinkingly the yellow-sapphire eyes stared at the rugged features. A trace of sound, so low and deep as to defy hearing, rumbled in the chest of the outlaw dog. His muzzle dropped ever so little. The pink tongue ran softly out, flicked the brown cheek once, twice.

Jim stirred uneasily, came abruptly awake, and sat bolt upright. Unconsciously his hand went to his cheek, came away moist. He sat a moment in the dark, uncomprehending.

Something was in the room with him—something that wasn't moving, that was waiting just as he was. There was that feeling that tells a man of the presence of another breathing being, although he can neither see nor hear anything. Gradually Jim's eyes absorbed the darkness, and the room became gray with the starlight.

It was empty. There was nothing in it.

At that moment the slender form of Bini, the she-cub, twitched convulsively where she lay on the foot of the rancher's bed. Jim was on his feet instantly, leaping clear of the bed and striking a match all in one motion.

He stared in fascination at the huddled puppy, with still more fascination at the two clear footprints on the clean bed-spread—one at either side of the pup's gaunt form—that indicated, as though in writing, the manner of her coming.

"Wolf-Eye," the man breathed softly, and, as though in faraway confirmation of his suppressed whisper, a deep, incredibly sad howl came mourning across the hushed grasses of Cedar Flats.

In no language on earth could Wolf-Eye have said good bye more plainly.

XII

"THE RED FLAME OF MADNESS"

Turning from his last look at Wolf Creek Ranch, Wolf-Eye swung into the tireless trot of the shepherd breed. Mile after mile he followed the brawling course of Wolf Creek downward across Cedar Flats. In a half hour's time he came to a point where Wolf Creek was joined by a smaller stream, the south fork of the Wolf, called Little Wolf.

Leaving the main stream, Wolf-Eye followed the Little Wolf toward the hills. He slowed his gait now, for the going was steeper.

Presently he paused. Above him towered twin monoliths of red granite, the Portal Rocks, age-old guardians of the issuance of the Little Wolf from its deep mountain cañon. The left-bank rock, the one that faced Wolf-Eye, was somewhat less tall and flatter-topped than its mate. The big dog's searching gaze scanned upward along the face of the granite giant. Toward the top a great scar cut across the rock's façade. In the width of this scar lay a jumble of small boulders and scrub juniper. This was the meeting place. This was where Vega and the cubs should be waiting for him.

Accessible only by an inches-wide trail from either the top or the bottom, it formed an impregnable retreat in times of danger and an ideal council chamber for pack gatherings. Wolf-Eye threw back his head and uttered a short howl. Immediately he was answered from above. Vega and the cubs were at the meeting place. Wolf-Eye howled again, and this time there was in the howl a note that told the ones waiting above to come down from their lofty rendezvous—that he, Wolf-Eye, would await them below. Vega howled back. It was understood. They were coming.

The dog sat down to wait. Now, with ten minutes' grace, he must somehow summon the will and strength to stalk and kill a grown steer. He drank a little of the cold water of the creek and lay down in the damp sand. A grateful calm stole over him. His eyelids drooped, gradually closed. Taut muscles slackened; nerve tensions were released. Wolf-Eye slept.

He awoke to find Vega standing over him. Behind her the pups crowded in an anxious, whimpering group. The she-wolf growled, and Wolf-Eye wearily, stiffly, came to his feet and growled in answer.

The group moved off, the dog in the lead, the she-wolf following, the cubs strung out behind her. He quickened the pace. Soon the pack was moving across open grassland. The way led downward and out from the mountain.

In a quarter of an hour Wolf-Eye called a halt, signaled Vega and the pups to come up with him. Snaking forward on their bellies, they joined him where he crouched peering from a thick tangle of juniper. Ahead lay an open meadow. In it were nearly fifty head of Hereford beef steers, their red and white forms bulking black in the moonlight. The pups stirred nervously, and Wolf-Eye shot them a hard glance of warning. These range-bred steers could run like deer and fight like lions; they were as wary as antelope and as uncertain as grizzlies. What they would do if alarmed was unpredictable. They might flee like cottontails or charge like buffalo. In the latter case, hunger-weakened as they were, some or all of the pack would find themselves under the knife-sharp hoofs.

The she-wolf watched without taking her cold eyes from the cattle. Finally she curled her lip in a low groan and backed cautiously out of the cover. Without hesitation five of the pups followed her. Only Rakar hesitated. Wolf-Eye turned on the recalcitrant cub and eyed him frostily. A silent lip lifted over inch-and-a-half fighting fangs. Rakar withdrew and padded hurriedly after his dam.

The plan was simple. Vega and the pups were to draw back into the rocks and lie low while Wolf-Eye circled the cattle downward and got on the far side of them. Then, after sufficient time, Vega was to work upwind of the herd. The moment the cattle got the wolf scent they would come to their feet. At this second Vega and the pups were to show themselves and make a great pretense of attack. Wolf-Eye calculated that the sight and sound and smell of Vega and the six cubs would be too much for the cattle and that they would bolt the meadow.

The lower end of the grassy arena was the natural exit. Here a fallen pine jutted out from the hillside and made a perfect place of concealment for Wolf-Eye.

Vega waited until there could be no doubt of her mate's readiness, then put the plan into action. Yammering like gray demons, the six cubs bore down upon the sleeping herd. In the van raced Vega, reckless in her hunger. Behind his log Wolf-Eye gathered his wasted haunches under him, kept his eyes glued to the cattle.

As the howling wolves burst from the rocks, the herd came to its feet as one. Wild-eyed, the steers stared at their attackers, hesitated an instant, then broke. Heads high, tails stiff, wattles clacking like machine-gun fire, they bore down on Wolf-Eye's ambush. The dog selected one of the smaller animals and attacked. His timing was perfect, and his teeth sliced through soft flesh to meet with a grinding jar in the steer's jugular. There was a ripping sound as the dog's momentum carried him beyond his victim. The stricken animal stumbled two steps and went down in a dead heap.

Wolf-Eye got to his feet. Blood spattered his silvery chest, ran from his black jowls. His eyes burned a deep orange. With a snarl he hurled himself on the dead steer. He had the work of disemboweling done before Vega and the pups could come up. He turned to greet them, his face a bloody mask. The hot flesh of the kill, the black, salty blood, the reaction from the past weeks of hunger, all served to accentuate the primal beast.

The pups tore rapidly at the steaming carcass. Only Vega hesitated a moment, eyeing Wolf-Eye strangely. The madness of the kill seemed to have unsettled him. She shook her head in puzzlement, then fell to feeding ravenously.

The flame in the great shepherd's eyes smoldered on. Snapping and snarling and grunting, he gorged on the sweet flesh of the young steer.

XIII
"THE CATTLE KILLINGS"

"Up by Portal Rocks, eh, Dave?"

"Yeah, Jim." The voice of the rancher's foreman, Dave Vail, was solemn. "I rode across the critter and thought you'd be interested."

"I'm plenty interested," said Jim tersely. "Let's move on up there."

They rode at an easy canter out across Cedar Flats. When they reached Little Wolf Creek, they turned upstream along the bank.

Halfway up to Little Wolf, Jim spoke. "Do you really think it was Wolf-Eye did the killin', Dave?"

"No way of tellin', boss. The kill's a month old and picked clean. There's a million coyote tracks laid over everything. Only reason I figured a wolf in the deal at all is that the critter's neck and foreleg bones was all fractured up like from a fall, only there wasn't any place to fall from. If it had died natural, there'd have been no broke bones. But, as far as the dog goes, I can't see no reason for suspectin' him special."

A careful study of the steer's remains showed nothing new. Jim agreed with his foreman. The beef *had* been killed. The killer might be wolf, lion, or bear. Most likely it had been wolves.

"Any way of tellin' whose beef it was?" asked Jim. "Did you find any hide?"

"Found enough. It was a K-Bar steer."

"Anything else been found?" asked the rancher.

"Shorty spotted two bunches of buzzards circlin' over on the south side of Wildcat. I'm sendin' him over there in the mornin'."

"Probably two separate kills."

"Probably."

"With the birds still circlin', there's a good chance they're fresh kills. If either of them is, let me know."

"Sure thing, boss," agreed Vail. "We'll get a line on this thing pretty soon. Shorty'll most likely find somethin' over there."

They rode home in silence. Jim's thoughts were with the distant Wolf-Eye. He had let the problem of Wolf-Eye's degeneration run along. But the return of the dog with the pitifully wasted female cub had brought the rancher hard up against the full facts. Cattle killer or no, the thought of a litter of wolves being reared under the leadership of the cattle-trained dog was one to bring any stockman into a cold sweat. Entering the home-pasture gate, he spoke to his foreman.

"Dave, I want to see Shorty the minute he gets back from Wildcat tomorrow. And send another good man with him. I want the right of this thing."

"Check," said Dave Vail. "I'll send Montana with him. He can read signs like an Indian."

The following day the 'puncher, Shorty, and his comrade, Montana, returned with the news that they had found two more steer carcasses, the first a big Rafter-CK two-year-old, the second a Lazy-T-Cross mossback. One kill was nearly two weeks old, the other less than a week. Both were too messed up to enable the 'punchers to check any details as to how they had died. There were plenty of wolf and coyote signs all around, but no dog track that they could positively identify.

That night brought news of yet another and fresher kill. Bill Edwards, a rancher from the far side of Wildcat, had found one of his old Triangle-E cows dead on the range, her carcass still warm.

"She died of throat trouble," vouchsafed the visiting rancher. "Brought on by an attack of wolfitis."

Jim rode back with Edwards the next day to examine the carcass. The creature was lying in the bottom of a dry gulch, her head obscured by a clump of mesquite. Without a word Jim swung down from his mount and pushed the screening clump of brush aside. His face twitched. Putting the toe of his boot under the dead cow's nose, he gave the head a flip. It flopped to one side, almost clear of the carcass. It was severed from ear to ear.

"What do you make of it?" drawled Edwards interestedly. "Wolf?"

"Dog," answered Jim through his teeth.

"You mean *your* dog? The shepherd you had that ran off?"

"Yes." The rancher's voice was tense. "He ran off with a red she-wolf last fall. They've got a litter of pups comin' a year old. The dog brought one of them into the ranch a month ago . . . sick, starved to death. She died after a week or so. He's killin' now to keep the rest of them goin'."

"What do you aim to do?" grunted Edwards.

"Only one thing to do," answered Jim slowly. "You round up the boys over on your side of Wildcat and drop over to the ranch soon as you're ready. Have them bring along beddin' and tack for several days. I'll furnish the grub."

"I'll do that," grunted Edwards.

"We can lose our shirts if that dog of mine brings those

pups through another winter," Jim added. "I'm convinced the dog has done all the killin' so far. But by next year the pups will be hard-grown and *trained*."

"Never thought of that angle," muttered Edwards. "You're sure right, though. With the trainin' that dog has passed on to them cubs . . . holy smoke!"

The two men were silent for a moment, each thinking his own thoughts. Then Jim, after a last look at the dead cow, swung into his saddle.

"See you tomorrow, Bill," he nodded.

"Good enough," answered his tight-mouthed companion.

XIV
"DEATH COMES TO THE SHE-WOLF"

It was late afternoon when Jim got back to the ranch. He unsaddled and turned his bay into the corral. As the horse kicked up and pranced away, Jim looked after it thoughtfully. This was the horse that had taken the kick at Wolf-Eye long ago. This was the horse he had ridden that day he laid out the trail for the shepherd puppy to follow. This was the horse he had been on the day Wolf-Eye had killed the Brahma. As the mind of the rancher reviewed these events, it seemed to keep repeating: *How long, long ago these things were! How quickly something that actually happened can become nothing but a memory?*

The red winter sun was settling into the saddle of granite connecting the two Portal Rocks. The brief Arizona twilight was deepening. Still Jim did not go into the ranch house. Instead, he wandered out to the corral where long ago Wolf-Eye had tripped up the Brahma steer. Standing in the snow-filled gateway, Jim saw again the assembled ranchers, felt again the sting of the tears in his eyes as Wolf-Eye had come to him and licked his cheek after killing the steer. The early moon caught the glint of moisture on the weathered cheek before the rancher could dash it hastily away.

Turning toward the house, the tall man paused by the woodpile and chuckled aloud. Among the chunks of cedar and piñon nestled several sections of smoothly rounded oak that looked very much like the remains of a wagon tongue. *Well, I reckon old Garcia would be runnin' yet if those ponies of his hadn't come a cropper on him. Man, how he lit out when he banged up against Wolf-Eye in that kitchen!*

Still chuckling, Jim hesitated by the kitchen door and, reaching up to a niche above it, brought down a folded piece of dirty blue denim. He spread this out and regarded it in silence. It was about a foot square and had edges that were ripped and frayed clear around. It was a hip pocket—the hip pocket out of the seat of Juan Garcia's blue denims. Jim put the fragment of cloth in his pocket and went into the ranch house. Behind him the moon eased over the adobe wall surrounding the yard.

Inside, Jim went to his room and sat down on the bed without making a light. Absent-mindedly he put his hand on the spot where Wolf-Eye used to sleep. As his big fingers stroked the bed coverings, his eyes wandered to the window.

If only you hadn't gone through that window that night, Wolfie! he mused. *If only you never had!*

Outside, the moon was as bright as phosphorus, drenching the ranch yard with its brilliance. Over by the far wall Jim could see the twisted cedar under which Wolf-Eye had established his outdoor bedroom. Here, sun or moonlight, the big shepherd had taken his ease. The prying light of the moon shouldered in under the branches of Wolf-Eye's cedar, revealing yet another reminder of the gray dog. In the middle of Wolf-Eye's bed of earth rose a small mound of banked dirt. At one end of it a small wooden cross was implanted. Upon the cross, carefully cut with Jim's jackknife, were the words:

Little Wolf-Eye

Bini, the she-cub, rested in peace where her father had slept before her.

Jim turned away from the window, wandered into the living room. He had laid a fire there that morning, and now he lit it. As the fire gathered strength, he slumped into his old Morris chair. His slippers lay unnoticed on the bookshelf from which Wolf-Eye had always brought them. Occasionally, as the fire died and the hours ticked away, Jim would stretch out his foot and move it in the air, back and forth as though in a scratching motion. He seemed not to notice, when he did this, or to realize that he sometimes dropped his right hand down past the side of the Morris chair and moved it gently in half-patting movements through the empty air.

When the fire was no more than a fitful tongue of smoky flame and long after the outside cold had penetrated the room, the rancher shook himself and stood up. The mantel clock stirred its rusty innards to begin the labor of striking three. It was still carrying out this ritual when the door of Jim's bedroom closed softly behind him.

In the weeks that followed, the bandit dog's toll mounted steadily. Soon the pace of the killings reached three a week. An intense campaign of traps, guns, and poison brought no result.

Wolf-Eye kept aloof, hunting alone and at night. When he killed for the pack, the female and the cubs did the driving. This tagging of the dog as the prime killer was largely established by his peculiar manner of throat slicing. It was his trademark—his signature.

The whims of fate had smiled on the dog and his savage brood. Since their first cattle kill the family had changed from gaunt ghosts to full-bodied creatures of flesh and substance. The six sons were magnificent specimens. Their black and red coats gleamed with health. Watching them move along the mesa trails, their wicked flat-skulled wolf heads held low and swinging slowly in the rhythm of their movement, even an untutored observer could have understood the apprehension of the ranchers.

At the same time Wolf-Eye became increasingly savage. He killed now for pleasure and for blood, not for food. His lot was cast with the wolves and against mankind. He felt, however, no inner satisfaction with this gory course. In the dog's heart there was no peace. In his mind, no rest. Dog that he was by blood, he could find no comfort in outlawry against his master's kind, nor, wolf that he now was by deed, could he show any allegiance to humanity.

In action and blood he found his only surcease from memory. Gradually he grew to associate this demon of his conscience with his memories of his wonderful early life with Jim. In his simple canine mind he knew only that his once great love for the man seemed to be forever intruding itself in his present course of crime. He sensed that killing cattle was an offense punishable only by death. It is the one sin from which a stock dog knows no redemption. The fact that his haunting memories of Jim would not let him sleep in peace while he persisted in his killings led gradually to a confusion in the dog's mind—a confusion in which he began to associate Jim with his present deep trouble. As the killing flame rose higher within him, burning out the last bridges of reason, he came finally to blame his master for everything. From here it was but a short step to a full-fledged hatred of all mankind. Wolf-Eye took this step without once pausing in his wild stride. The rate of his insane killings rose constantly.

Vega, her natural fear of man greatly lessened by her shepherd mate's disdain of him, took to hunting in broad daylight. The ease with which her dog mate slew the steers dulled the she-wolf's instincts. In a short time she was roaming the Wildcat ranges with abandon. The fact that she and her vicious band were the objects of one of the Southwest's biggest wolf hunts did not seem to deter her. Certainly she was aware of the pursuit, but she ignored it. With her in her flagrant way traveled the six sons.

Jim and his foreman were riding to the scene of the pack's latest kill. With them was a Cattle Association hunter. It was early morning. A light breeze blew in their faces. The ground under the horses' hoofs was soft and springy. The men had not spoken for several minutes.

Topping a rise, they uttered sudden oaths. Vail's horse and that of the Association hunter bolted. Jim was out of his saddle and clear of his mount before that dumbfounded creature could move. On one knee now, with his .30-30 traveling toward his shoulder, the big rancher crouched. Not fifty feet away, seven wolves paused, snarling in their tracks.

Six of them dived instantly for the cover of a deep wash just behind them. Into this haven they vanished as if by magic. The seventh hesitated a split second, confused. Then it, too, sprang for cover. The .30-30 echoed flatly. It was not a difficult shot for a rifleman like Jim. The morning sun was at his back, the wind true in his face, the range pointblank. Vega's form twisted in mid-air as the bullet smashed into her ribs. The impact carried her over the lip of the wash and into the brush below.

The men followed her as quickly as they could.

"Don't see how in the name of Satan she made it off," whistled Jim, examining the bright trail of frothy blood. "She's shot through both lungs, I'll bet my bottom dollar."

"She's lung shot, all right." The Association hunter's words were tight, professional. "You can tell that by the froth

Will Henry

and the light-red color of the blood."

"She won't get far," opined Dave Vail.

Nevertheless, a half hour's trailing failed to bring them up
with the she-wolf. Another ten minutes and Jim called a halt.

"Well, boys, that's a wolf for you. Shot to death and
doesn't know it."

"More infernal cussedness than a government mule,"
agreed the foreman laconically.

"How about gettin' my dogs on the trail?" asked the Association man. "We can find the she-wolf's body that way, and
then set up a watch by it. The cubs are bound to come
around."

"Maybe you're right," answered Jim. "It's a gamble any
way. Even if it's night, when they come around, we might get
a snap shot or two at them . . . up close."

"Wolf-Eye might even drop around to shed a tear," said
Dave Vail grimly.

Lop Ear brought the news to Wolf-Eye where the latter lay
in a birch thicket still resting from the preceding night's kill.
Whining excitedly, the big cub urged Wolf-Eye to follow him.
The dog, sensing the cub's fear, was at once on his feet.
Swiftly the young wolf and his shepherd-dog sire raced for the
dying she-wolf.

In a few minutes they neared Vega's resting place. Lop Ear
indicated her position as they approached. Wolf-Eye noted it,
then snarled rapidly at the cub. The big youngster snarled in
reply and, after a moment, turned and made his way back
toward the home den. He had been ordered to gather the
pack, and he would do it. Of all the cubs, Wolf-Eye trusted
only Lop Ear, the Foolish One.

When the cub had gone, Wolf-Eye slipped quietly
around the boulders that Lop Ear had pointed out to him.

He came at once upon his stricken mate.

At his arrival she opened her eyes, summoned the will to move her head a little and to whimper softly. She was far gone.

As Wolf-Eye growled and crouched at her side, a black shadow floated across the sunlit grasses. The dog turned his head skyward to snarl at the drifting buzzard. As he did so, the first shadow was joined by a second—and a third. Wheeling noiselessly, they cruised backward and forward, upwind and down.

Wolf-Eye, with the greatest care, dragged the dying she-wolf into the protection of a nearby rock group. Vega had instinctively made for water and in her agony had almost reached it. The big shepherd found a thin seepage collected in a two-foot pool at the base of the largest boulder. Vega drank weakly. Wolf-Eye licked her shattered side and snapped at the invading flies. The she-wolf's eyes acknowledged her gratitude. Gradually the pain went out of them. Feebly she raised her head, letting it fall on her mate's outstretched forepaw. Wolf-Eye rumbled deeply in his chest, a tone of misery and pleading love. His tongue caressed the beautiful she-wolf's slim muzzle. She answered with a like caress. The dog lay his great head beside her slender one. Vega sighed deeply and relaxed. Somewhere inside her tortured body a final hemorrhage occurred. The she-wolf died in peace, and painlessly.

XV

"THE KILLER AT BAY"

As the great dog stood over the still-warm corpse of his mate, the last veneer of civilization withered from him. For a long minute he gazed toward the valley down the gorge through which Vega had struggled to reach her beloved hills. The rising afternoon wind brought a sudden chill upon the hillside. From below, borne upward on the new air, came the sudden bawling of a trailing hound. In a moment other voices joined the opening one. The sound became the wild music of a hound pack in full cry.

Wolf-Eye threw back his head and howled. It was a strange howl, loaded with anger and sadness.

Hearing it, Jim Lewis turned to his companions. "There he is, boys," he said, and, as he spoke, there was a certain fierce pride in his voice. "That's Wolf-Eye!"

"Reckon you know your own dog," answered the hunter, "but he sure sounds like a wolf to me."

"Sounds mad to me," observed Dave Vail soberly.

"I believe the she-wolf's dead." The Wolf Creek rancher's voice was low. "That howl didn't come from any happy heart."

The three men fell silent as the floor of the gorge steepened beneath their laboring mounts. Above them a sudden snarling and yelping broke out. The clamor was fierce—desperate.

"C'mon, boys!" yelled Vail. "That ain't any ordinary fuss."

"You reckon that's the dogs pitchin' on the she-wolf?" asked Jim, reining up his excited mount.

"Not with that noise!" exploded the hunter, already spurring his horse up the wash. "Those dogs aren't pitchin' on anything . . . they're getting pitched on!"

At the end of his howl Wolf-Eye turned to go. Below him the clamor of the hounds drew nearer. With the dogs would come the men and, with the men, guns. There was no more to be done here. The big shepherd started up the draw. As he did so, the hounds broke across a clear space in the trail below.

Wolf-Eye checked instinctively and watched them come streaming upward. One, two, three, four of them. Big brutes. Three hounds and an Airedale-cross, tonguing and yelling like mad. Something in their howling eagerness seared the big dog's conscience. They were coming to tear at his dead mate—to defile his red she-wolf.

Wolf-Eye saw red. The lust to kill was upon him. Soundlessly he faded into the tall grasses, crouched there, and lay still. Only the stem of a sumac seedling swayed to show where one hundred and twenty-five pounds of fire-eyed murder trembled and waited.

The hounds came struggling up the last grade. Before them lay the body of Vega, the she-wolf. Fresh blood was spattered about the scene of her death. Aroused by the sight of the helpless enemy, the hounds bore down on the huddled carcass. In their lead went the Airedale-cross, his terrier blood eager for the worrying of the prey.

As they reached the she-wolf's body, the very mountainside appeared to explode in their faces. A huge black and silver dog burst into their midst like a fur bombshell. One hound was dead and another down before the mêlée was five seconds old. Yammering excitedly, the Airedale closed with Wolf-Eye. True to his terrier's heart, he knew no fear. But he fought alone. The wounded hound would never fight again, and the uninjured one was screaming down the cañon in full flight.

The Airedale died fighting. He was a brave dog and a powerful one, but Wolf-Eye was berserk. The game terrier was literally torn to ribbons. He stumbled blindly and fell, still whimpering, still eager for the fray. Wolf-Eye stood and watched him die.

Downcañon arose the sound of shod hoofs on rock and the grunting of men's voices. Wolf-Eye scrambled up the steep side of the gorge and threaded his way through the hillside boulders. In a moment he was lost to view. Seconds later Jim and his companions came up the final grade and stood in sight of the carnage. The hunter dragged the surviving dog by a steel lead chain. When the slinking animal came up to his dead comrades, he broke into a frenzy of fear. The hunter choked him short with the sliding chain.

"Good grief, boys!" said Dave Vail simply. "Look at that Airedale."

Jim said nothing, his eyes traveling quickly over the whole scene.

"Give me your six-gun," said the hunter flatly. "That brown hound's done for."

Jim handed him the gun.

The shot echoed sharply. The hunter handed the revolver back to the rancher. "I'll get that black-faced devil for this." He spoke softly. "I'll get him if it's the last thing I do."

"That's right, Dave," Jim agreed with his foreman. "We've got to get him quick now."

"Looks like he stood them off to keep them from gettin' at the female's body, eh, boss?"

"Looks that way."

"Mighty good job he did of it."

"Mighty good dog," countered the rancher grimly.

"He'll be good and dead when I get through with him," muttered the hunter. "Good and *dead*."

Jim had no way of knowing how violent the reaction from Vega's death would be, but he knew the dog's loneliness would seek an active outlet. He was afraid that outlet would prove to be an increased destruction of range stock, a blood purge. He was not long in having his fear confirmed.

Through February and early March—Vega had died in January—the rate of killings rose enormously. Some, now, were the work of the cubs, but eight in ten bore the bloody trademark of the master himself—the gaping half-moon slash from ear to ear. These carcasses were for the most part untouched. Big prime steers had been wantonly destroyed by the dozen. In one night alone five grown beeves fell to Wolf-Eye's crazy campaign. They were found at points stretching over thirty miles of rough rangeland, in itself an indication of the restless madness of the killer. As though the inflamed brain of the dog was not enough, the cubs soon caught the insanity of his mood and began to join in the pointless slaughter. More and more uneaten carcasses were found scattered across the Wildcat range. In the end the toll stood at bankruptcy rates for the ranchers.

The time for spotty effort was far past. The entire Mogollon rangeland erupted into action. Seventeen members assembled at Wolf Creek Ranch. Four Biological Survey men from three Southwestern states were present. The Association sent in a new pack of fourteen fighting cross-lion and wolf hounds. With the pack came an Isleta Indian trailer who could follow a pack rat's tracks across flint rock. With him would work old Juan Garcia, Jim's ranch cook, a famous tracker in his day. These two would take up any trail the hounds were unable to follow by reason of impassable terrain.

The morning set for the final hunt came, cold and windy with a fine drizzle slanting in from the northeast. Trailing conditions were perfect, with both air and ground damp. The dogs were eager, the men ready.

And the trail was fresh! Two cowboys had been coming in to Wolf Creek from an outlying line camp. Finding themselves within half a night's ride of the home ranch when darkness came on, they had decided to ride on through. They had taken their time over supper and got started about eight o'clock. There was a bright moon and a clearing sky after an afternoon bluster of snow and rain. The ground was soft and springy underfoot, and they had traveled without much talk. At one o'clock in the morning they were topping out behind Portal Rocks, about five miles from the ranch. They reined up astonished. Ahead of them six black wolves and a huge gray dog were tearing at a freshly killed carcass of beef.

Following their brush with Wolf-Eye and his wolf cubs the cowboys had ridden hard for the ranch. There they had told their story to Jim, who had immediately dispatched riders to arouse the neighboring ranchers. The latter had ridden in all during the night hours, until by 5:00 A.M. everybody was assembled, in saddle, and ready to go. The entire tight-jawed crew rode off into the thick dawn a few minutes after five o'clock.

The start from the carcass was made about six. The hounds took the trail at once and worked off in a southeasterly direction up and around the lower side of Wildcat. After a few minutes' trailing, the hounds doubled back and ran a trail straight down to Portal Rocks. Here the quarry had drifted downstream. The trail was broad and clear, the scent hot and heavy. The hounds raced along it, their bugle voices running a full scale of wild bawlings.

XVI
"THE MASTER PLAN"

Wolf-Eye loped easily along in the van of his killer sons. Tongue lolling, muscles rolling, head swinging, he was the picture of nonchalance. But his quick brain was racing with the speed of light. He knew that at last he had blundered. His leadership had failed. It galled him to think he had been tripped up by pure accident, forced to leave a hot trail because some stupid humans had stumbled across him in a night ride.

He held his course until the twin bulks of Portal Rocks loomed ahead. Then he swung left to lead the pack downstream. Rakar immediately broke into a snarl of challenge. A wolf will always break for higher ground. The other cubs joined in Rakar's snarls.

Wolf-Eye's answer was to turn downstream without further growling. The cubs followed silently. Now they were beginning to grow uneasy. They sensed for the first time that they were in trouble. Wolf-Eye felt their anxiety and shared it with them. They were right. There was great danger. At Wolf Creek Ranch a new pack of dogs had gathered. They were not like the slow hounds that Wolf-Eye had slain in the cañon of his mate's death. These had the look of hunters and fighters. They were lean and fit, and they had been given a hot, clear trail. There was the greatest danger. The trail was too hot. The hounds' voices would be heard before the day

102

was an hour over the mountain.

The cubs fell silent, each with his own thoughts, all deeply disturbed. Something they had never known crawled along their spines, settled with a chill behind their shoulders. Their first fear was upon them.

The mind of the wolf dog cross-balances narrowly on the brink of insanity, at best. The splendid brain of the dog is often contaminated with the germ of the wolf's cold ferocity. Hybrid animals appear to be notoriously nervous and uncertain, and Wolf-Eye's sons were no exception. Like fire the fear virus leaped through their veins. By the time they reached the juncture of the Wolf and Little Wolf, their tempers were running out of hand. But Wolf-Eye paid them no heed. His was the authority here, and his the responsibility of leadership. Quickly he thought of his plan.

The joining of the Wolf and Little Wolf creeks lay just ahead. There they would separate. Wolf-Eye would go on from there alone. The sons would follow the Little Wolf up through Portal Rocks. Beyond the rocks men and horses could not go. The cubs would continue through the cañon of the Little Wolf into the high country of the mountain. The men would certainly guess their course, once they had seen the cubs' trail going into the cañon. Then the men would go across country and around Portal Rocks to the headwaters of the Little Wolf. This would take them late into the day. With any good speed the cubs would be past the headwaters and out of the cañon well before the men could arrive there.

Once through the cañon, the cubs would go on around the south slope of Wildcat. Where they came out, it would be high—and the surrounding country would be one of bare rock, with the snow yet heavy within it. They would have to travel north, up the far side of Wildcat. The hounds by that time should be very weary. But the cubs were wolves, and they would still be strong. They would be a full hour ahead of the horsemen who were coming around Portal Rocks. They would travel until they reached Icy Meadow, and there Wolf-Eye would meet them. The shepherd himself would go by the north fork of the Wolf, through Cedar Flats, across the place that once was his home, and thus into the north cañon of the Wolf. At first, upon leaving the cubs, he would travel in the water of the stream while they traveled by its bank. In this way they could make certain that the hounds would follow the cubs through the south cañon. All that would remain for Wolf-Eye would be to stay ahead of the men who followed him and to gain, if he could, an hour on them to match the hour the cubs would gain on the dogs.

He and the cubs would come to Icy Meadow in nice time to take care of the dogs. The hounds would be only minutes behind the cubs, but there could be a little time for rest, even so. There would be no trouble. The men would be far behind on both trails, and there was no need to worry about them. The whole business of finishing the dogs would be short and very pleasant.

With the dogs dead, Wolf-Eye and his sons could cross back over the summit of Wildcat, thus eluding the men. Horses could not come even so far as Icy Meadow, and the men, on foot, would abandon the hunt when they saw the wolves had cut back over the mountain.

The cubs snarled ready agreement to the plan. Some of the madness of flight and fear had left them during Wolf-Eye's cool thinking. They now sensed the wisdom and soundness of the big dog's leadership. Four among them, Akhab, Sonjii, Barek, and Korok, understood that failure meant death. The thistle-witted Lop Ear was unable to comprehend anything beyond the general excitement and fun of being chased, while the murderous Rakar still was of a silent mind to do battle before the Icy Meadow rendezvous.

With short snarls Wolf-Eye sent them on their way. The pack swung sullenly into the stream and quartered across it diagonally. On the far bank they turned upstream and fell into the high lope of the traveling wolf. In a moment they were out of sight.

Wolf-Eye watched them go. Then, with a grunt of satisfaction, he plunged into the swift waters of Wolf Creek and began his own long upstream journey.

It happened as Wolf-Eye had figured it would—up to a point. The hounds came squalling to the creek junction twenty minutes after the shepherd dog and his six wolf sons had left it. They swung unerringly cross-stream where the cubs' tracks entered. On the far side they fanned out and circled. The fighting dogs splashed across in their wake and stood waiting for the hounds to pick up the trail.

One of the hounds tongued from a spot upstream. Immediately the other dogs rushed toward the sound, and in a moment the pack was yammering in rhythm. The scent was hot and sweet, and the hounds bawled with the excitement of it. The heavy wolf scent was like fire in their delicate nostrils. Behind them the fighting cross-dogs snarled and yelled their impatience.

Shortly after the pack, the men came up. In their lead was Jim Lewis and the Association hunter. At their backs rode the Indian tracker and old Juan Garcia. As Wolf-Eye had thought, his obvious ruse was unraveled.

"Boys," called Jim as the other ranchers reined up, "unless I'm greatly mistaken, Wolf-Eye split up the pack here. He's done it purposely to divide us and the dogs. You can bet he's put the dogs after the cubs, and he's lit off on the lonesome trail."

"OK, Jim," answered one of the men. "It's your dog, and it's your picnic. What's the deal?"

"Thanks, Charlie. Here's the setup the way it grades up to me. Wolf-Eye is off alone. There's no tracks, so he's wadin' either downstream of the south fork here or upstream of the north fork over yonder."

"My guess is the main branch. The north fork there, upstream," put in the Association hunter.

"Mine, too," answered Jim. "The south fork would run him out on the Flats, where he wouldn't have a chance. He's too smart for that. He's gone upstream and back into the hills. That will put him on the north slope of Wildcat, and the young ones on the south slope. He and the cubs are probably plannin' a get-together over there on the far side somewhere."

"What do you aim to do, Jim?" asked Clay Peters.

"Well, Clay," continued Jim, "while you boys are makin' your run for the head of the south fork, I'm goin' to send the Indian tracker and the Association hunter up the north fork on whatever trail Wolf-Eye leaves us there. I'll go right over the top of Wildcat . . . make up nearly an hour on him that way. He's only a dog, and he can't have thought of everything. He's pretty sure to be thinkin' he's got part of us on his trail and part on the cubs'. He won't figure much deeper than that. Comin' over the top of the mountain, I ought to get between him and his cubs before they can get together. Maybe I can anyway. It's a good chance. If I can get a shot at the dog before he gets together with the cubs, we're goin' to be savin' ourselves a lot of trouble. He's the brains of the outfit, and without him the others will be easy. But once he gets back with the cubs, and what with night shuttin' down on us, we'll have a bad time followin' the dogs. He's goin' to be in high country on the other side . . . plenty of rock and snow. It'll be tough. Now, then, we're goin' to have to step on it to get over the mountain by dark. Any questions?"

"Sounds like as good a deal as any," offered the senior government hunter. "I'll lead the boys on the south fork end of it, if you want."

"Good. Let's all get goin' then."

XVII
"CORNERED"

Rakar trailed the pack up the south fork cañon. Behind him now could be heard the cry and straining of the pack. Rakar's roach stood on end as he ran. Yellow slaver flecked his chopping jaws, and his eyes burned green with madness. With Wolf-Eye gone and the noise of the dog pack close behind, fear came again to the cubs. It rode most strongly on Rakar, who was the most nervous and high-strung of the litter and who had never been afraid of anything in his life.

For several seconds he growled and snarled as they ran, and Lop Ear by turn listened seriously, yapped approval, growled deeply, or whimpered vacuously. When Rakar had done with his mouthings, the two wolf dogs dropped out of the pack and hung farther and farther back at each turn of the cañon. Akhab, the Brave, who led the way, saw them and flung them a snarled warning to keep up. Nevertheless, as the pack cleared the next turn, Rakar and the witless one were no longer with it.

Rakar and Lop Ear crouched, waiting for the hounds. In the Cruel One's mind the simple thing to do was to stop and fight the dogs. Rakar had never run from anything in his fierce life. He was not going to start now, Wolf-Eye or no Wolf-Eye. The traitorous cub and his foolish brother gathered their haunches under them. The hounds were just around the near bend.

With a roar Rakar leaped from concealment upon the astonished hounds. Like a lightning bolt the lean form of the black killer flashed forth between the two lead hounds. One! Two! He struck them, and, in less time than the words are written, they were gasping out their lives on the cañon floor. Turning to aid Lop Ear, Rakar's eyes widened with anger. The Foolish One had clumsily missed his charge, and the third hound was in free flight down the cañon. Worse yet, behind him went the lumbering Lop Ear, yapping and howling like a coyote chasing jack rabbits.

Impassively Rakar watched his brother turn a far corner in the cañon and disappear. There was a long minute's suspended hush, then a sudden uproar of wild snarls, growls, and wicked snappings. Lop Ear was among the ghosts of his people. Rakar turned and faded swiftly upcañon.

Now, through no fault of his own, Wolf-Eye's plan began to fall to pieces. In all, there were perhaps five minutes between the wolf pack's exit from the head of the south fork cañon and the mounted hunters' arrival there. Jim's counterplan had almost worked and had at very least cost the fugitives almost an hour of priceless time. In addition, the dog pack had cut deeply into the narrow margin of time safety Wolf-Eye had figured for the cubs to hold. The laboring, excited brutes burst from the cañon a scant ten minutes after the wolf pack. This put them within occasional sight of the cubs and brought them up to the hunters after their mounts had enjoyed a five-minute breather. Thus, not only had the cubs lost their advantage over the dogs, but the hunters were almost upon them instead of an hour behind them. Wolf-Eye's nicely balanced scheme was thrown completely off. Rakar's disaffection had paid dividends beyond his imagination.

In spite of the pack's hatred of Rakar, there was no murmur as the Cruel One took over the lead from Akhab. He had been their leader even while Vega was alive, and so it seemed only natural now for him to take over. Rakar was shrewd enough to realize the best chance lay in reaching Wolf-Eye. Accordingly he led the pack full-tilt across the high east slope of Wildcat. Gradually he opened up a distance between the cubs and the dogs. The latter, in turn, responded by increasing their lead over the hunters. Thus, as the chase neared Icy Meadow, conditions were slightly improved.

Wolf-Eye toiled up the last slope before Icy Meadow. At the crest he paused. Before him lay the half mile of the cup of the meadow, its brown winter grass and gaunt boulders sheathed in the crusty snow-ice of the high places. Wolf-Eye's deep breath stained the thin air in white cloud puffs. Behind him lay a two-mile climb across open country. He looked back. As yet there were no signs of pursuit. So far so good. He had an hour to spare. Choosing a sheltered spot between high boulders, he lay down to rest and to await the cubs.

Jim paused to blow. The climb over the backbone of Wildcat had been a tough one. He had left his horse at the timberline and come the last three miles on foot. The course had been almost straight up, but now he was topped out, and below him was the barren east side of Wildcat Mountain. Almost directly beneath his summit position lay Icy Meadow. He noticed that from the crest line to the meadow below tumbled a jagged, narrow rock cleft about two miles long. It was like a grand, craggy staircase leading from the upper meadow, up and over the crest of Wildcat Mountain. It thus formed the only feasible outlet from Icy Meadow.

Jim pulled his old silver watch from an inside pocket. It was five minutes to six. In another fifteen minutes the quick Arizona night would shut down. Already a fat white moon was climbing up out of the far Rockies. Taking his binoculars, the rancher flopped down on the granite ridge and studied the land below. At first he saw nothing. Then, as the glasses swung past Icy Meadow to the left, Jim uttered a grunt of satisfaction. Far below, a single figure toiled across the snow. It was unquestionably his long lost dog.

"Well, old son," the rancher muttered half aloud, "it looks like we out-figured you this time." Then as an afterthought: "Man alive, will you look at him! Good gosh!"

Jim had not seen Wolf-Eye since the night the young dog had left, nearly a year and a half ago. Now, as he watched the big shepherd approach Icy Meadow, a lump rose in his throat. He laid the glasses aside and wiped his eyes. *Damn this wind up here. Cuts into your eyes like a knife. Sure makes them water.*

He resumed his study through the glasses. Wolf-Eye had grown. He was immense now. His shoulders and haunches were heavy with muscle; his loin was as broad as a mastiff's, his legs thick as a Malamute's. His broad skull and wide jaw gave his head a look of dangerous potency. Yet, withal, such was the perfection of his movements, the depth and life of his winter pelt, the easy grace of his carriage, that the watcher had no sense of burliness or clumsiness. He was simply a huge, vicious-looking dog, as finely trained and conditioned as his hard life could make him. In the failing light Jim could make out only these general characteristics of the dog. Detail and close-up features were lost. Still, it was a long five minutes before the rancher laid aside the glasses.

In those five minutes Jim saw many things. A quick train of memory ran back and brought the dog swiftly to the lonely rocks of Icy Meadow. Here he was, run to his last earth,

111

backed to his last wall, ready to die in a bare, ugly saucer of rock two thousand feet above timberline, preparing to kill even as death came running on the heels of the hound pack, going to his death as he had lived, friendless and alone. Jim shook himself. *Brrr! The wind sure cut clean up here. Time to get moving.*

Far below he had seen Wolf-Eye bed down among the rocks and had guessed that he was awaiting the cub pack. Upon the next move depended the outcome of the far-flung chase. If the shepherd were to lead his sons out of the meadow by way of the staircase cleft over the crest line, the hunt would be over. Horses could not come even so far as the meadow, let alone negotiate the cleft's dizzy floor, while men on foot could not hope to keep up with the dogs in such steep and hazardous climbing.

Wolf-Eye had planned well, almost brilliantly. What he could not have foreseen was his former master's decision to cross the summit and come between him and his avenue of escape. Jim held the dog's life in his hand as surely as though he were holding a loaded revolver between the animal's sharp ears. The moment the rancher entered the upper end of the cleft, Wolf-Eye and his sons would be dead. There was no other outlet. Between the meadow and the summit the cleft ran hundreds of feet deep. The walls were perpendicular. By by-passing the cleft, working his way down its upper rim, the rancher could give his dog freedom and life.

Jim hesitated a moment, then, plunging and sliding, rifle held high to clear the deep snow, he began the treacherous descent. Straight into the cleft he went, and in a few minutes the black walls flanked him a hundred feet deep. The night was down hard by now, and the fat moon had labored clear of the mountains. Its white light poured in a flood over the snow-packed floor of the staircase cleft. Jim made good time.

XVIII
"THE ICY MEADOW TRAP"

Wolf-Eye stirred uneasily. The pack was overdue. Something had gone amiss. Many things were possible, and Rakar's desertion was the most likely. Wolf-Eye's lip curled. He had long known that between Rakar and him there must be an accounting. The cubs were now fifteen months old, grown in mind and body. Rakar was their natural leader. The wolf blood in him called to that in his brothers. Wolf-Eye, for all his cunning and savage killing, was a dog. Between the cubs and him there could never be that bond necessary for real leadership. They understood Rakar. With him they were in sympathy. He was a wolf.

Rakar was a fool concluded Wolf-Eye. When this business of the Icy Meadow trap was done, they would see how anxious the Cruel One was for leadership. Nevertheless, the thought of Rakar's disaffection was an uneasy one. The dog knew that, when Rakar turned, he would turn the pack with him. The law of the wolf pack was that combat could be joined only by the immediately interested parties, challenged and challenger. There was to be no help proffered to either side. One against one, and the winner to take all. If there is a canine action to match man's laughter, Wolf-Eye imitated it at that thought. He knew his sons better than that. Of the lot, only Lop Ear, with his clown's mind, could be discounted.

The others, including level-headed Sonjii, were unqualified killers. They would no more think of letting Rakar fight him singly than they would of individually fighting him themselves. They ran as a pack, and they would fight as a pack, notwithstanding the law of wolves to the contrary.

In effect Rakar had led them since before Vega's death. Wolf-Eye had been only the nominal head. They followed the dog from habit alone. No sense of duty or respect was involved. Wolf-Eye had avoided the final dispute for tactical reasons. He had awaited Rakar's move. He knew that the big cub held no fear of him. The move would surely come sooner or later.

Wolf-Eye thought, now, of these things and wondered what had befallen his savage brood. He was not without regard for them. At Vega's death he had turned to the cubs. In their coldness he had found some response to the new lust within himself, in their age-old hatred of mankind, sympathy for his newly born hatred. And he had felt the call of common blood, the bond of paternalism. The cubs, however, rejected this premise. They felt nothing, save perhaps the one cub Sonjii, for their sire. The split thus remained one-sided. The shepherd thought of the cubs as his sons, his flesh. They thought of him as a stranger, an imposed power, an interloper, a *dog*.

Suddenly Wolf-Eye's reverie was shattered. Down the mountainside there? Were his ears playing him tricks? No. There it came again—the bawling of a hound pack in full tune.

The giant shepherd was on his feet, hackles stiff, head high. The wind was strong away from him, and the voices of the hounds were coming against the wind. This meant they must be quite near, for the wind was rising, and the cubs were still heading them. This much he could tell by the tone of the dogs' baying. But apparently the youngsters held much less of a margin than he had planned.

Wolf-Eye's mind raced. He had blundered again. He should have taken Rakar with him. This lateness of the cubs was almost surely some work of his. However, there was little time for recrimination. The gray dog quivered. Across the meadow came his sons. But what was this? They were not running in good order. They were fleeing in wild disarray.

Rakar came first and at his flank, Akhab and Barek. Fifty feet behind them ran Korok, and far behind him, nearly a quarter mile, limped Sonjii. Even from the distance he could see that the cubs were in sore straits. Their flanks were sunken, their loins, pinched. In the stillness of a sudden pause in the wind, the dog could hear their explosive panting and gasping. Foam flecked their faces and streamed in thick slavers from their parted jaws.

Rakar panted up and flung himself on the ground. Barek and Akhab followed him. In a moment Korok joined them. Sonjii, still limping, struggled across the meadow. The hounds were not in sight, and for the time their voices were lost in the wind.

The big shepherd's growls took on a sudden depth of savagery as he interrupted the cubs' pantings to warn them they had no time for standing there slobbering. As if to punctuate his warning growl, the loud yammering of the hound pack burst with sudden nearness. The cubs leaped excitedly to their feet.

Wolf-Eye's deep growls went on without a break. He directed the cubs' attention to the staircase cleft. They all snarled their understanding. They were familiar with it. It led back over the mountain, was hard for men, impossible for horses. It was a good exit.

Akhab growled nervously. Those thrice-cursed dogs were

coming up faster than a new wind. Sonjii snarled hastily, and Barek and Korók started edging upmeadow toward the cleft. Only Rakar stood proud and disdainful. He would not show fear or nerves where the sire stood like a rock. Wolf-Eye snarled for the cubs to continue their flight. Without hesitation they did so, and after a moment Wolf-Eye followed them with the injured Sonjii.

Around the rim of the meadow's icebound edge, the four huge wolf dogs drifted with smoke-puff speed. They moved as though refreshed and strong.

Wolf-Eye and Sonjii set off up the center of the meadow, moving slowly. As they did so, the first of the eager dogs piled into the far side of the arena. Wolf-Eye grunted with satisfaction as he noted that Rakar and his crew were well out of sight.

Dark was closing down, and a cold moon rose up over the rim of Icy Meadow. A keen-eyed bull terrier fighting dog let out a yell of discovery and cut sharply toward the staggering pair of fugitives in mid-meadow. After him came the others, ten big rawboned fighting brutes, eager for the kill. Abandoned was the trail. No use for the nose here. This was sight-hunting, and the race was to the swift. The dogs ran like fiends, their bellies stretched to the snow.

XIX

"JIM'S GAMBLE"

Jim paused for breath halfway down the staircase cleft. The moon was directly overhead. A low bank of gray snow cloud was moving up sharply, and the rancher shivered as the thin mountain air whistled up the snow-choked cleft. Pulling his sheepskin higher about his ears, he started on down the steep declivity.

He didn't like this sky a bit. It was going to cover over the moon any minute now, and, when it did, the tortuous going of the cleft's boulder-blocked, ice-rimmed bottom would become doubly dangerous. With good light it wasn't too bad. But the walls here were hundreds of feet high and almost perpendicular. If the moon gave out, anything could happen.

As he rounded a sharp turn about a mile above Icy Meadow, he was met by a mêlée of snarling sounds borne up to him from the chill depths of the meadow. It was sounds of deep animal gutturals and high-pitched hound voices. The dogs had come up with the wolves! Clear above all the clambering rose one voice, deep and base and challenging.

"Wolfie!" The word burst from Jim's lips and echoed in the rock depths like a pistol shot. "By heaven, they've got him!"

Unslinging his Winchester and dumping his food pack in the snow, the rancher started down the cañon. Running, sliding, scrambling, he plunged eagerly toward the sound of the conflict. Apparently luck was with him. His guess had been good. The pack was headed up the staircase cleft.

Several things happened at once then. Afterward the rancher could remember none of them distinctly. The cañon grew abruptly dark as the moon dived under the thick edge of an oncoming snow cloud. He was running one moment in good white light, and the next he was falling in darkness. There was a single, spine-twisting jolt and a grinding, whirling halt. Snow and ice filled his eyes, ears, and mouth. He lay quietly, his mind numb with the shock of the fall. He moved his head a little and spat snow from his mouth. His right arm was free, and he brushed it across his eyes. Presently he could see.

He was lying in snow and loose rocks, wedged and jammed to the hips. His left leg was partially free and movable, his right he could neither see nor feel. He knew it was broken. His left arm hung bent at a grotesque angle between wrist and elbow. It gave no pain. Broken leg and arm, and blood all around, black against the white snow. He could taste its hot salt now, as sensation returned to his battered lips. He must have cut his face up pretty bad. Some fall, all right—a nasty one. He glanced up to see where he had come from.

Above him was an eight-foot-deep split in the trail, a natural V-shaped pitfall. Into this he had stepped at a full run. About four feet wide at the top, the split narrowed to nothing at the bottom. The fact that it was blocked with snow had broken Jim's fall and possibly saved him a broken neck or back. Yet, as it was, the picture wasn't any too good. He had two broken limbs and lay wedged, helpless, in the middle of the only remaining passage up the staircase cleft. And some of Wolf-Eye's cubs were on their way up!

The awkwardness of his position struck him instantly.

Good thing he had his right arm free and his .30-30 handy. He'd be in a bad spot otherwise. Some of the maddened pack below might fight clear of the dogs and retreat on up the cleft. In so doing they'd run smack onto rancher Jim Lewis. The big man grinned painfully and spat more blood. His hand felt in the snow for the cold assurance of the Winchester's barrel. If there was snow plugged in the bore, it was time to get it out now before the wolf crew showed up. They'd be in no mood to argue about trail rights with a pack of rough dogs and a dozen hunters on their heels.

The big cowman's shoulders brushed the steep rock walls of his narrow prison. The trail above fared smoothly into the sides of the chasm. A mountain goat couldn't have gotten past Jim without stepping squarely in his face. The rancher grimaced. He knew better than to place any reliance in the old hokum of wolves never attacking humans. Men had been killed by wolves before and would be again. Hunger is the usual goad, but fear will drive as hard a bargain. Those big half-breed brutes would as soon cut his throat as look at him, and especially with him helpless, blood-covered, and blocking their path to freedom. He felt deeper into the snow with his good right hand.

Then he knew the rifle wasn't there. In a moment he remembered—a flash of the familiar short, thick-barreled carbine whirling through the air, the sting of the blow on the granite outcropping that had sheared it from his hand. Frantically he tore at the snow, buried his arm in it to the shoulder, stretched it full-length in every direction. The carbine was gone. It might be a few feet away, inches under the snow. It might as well be in the rack above the mantel at Wolf Creek Ranch. In spite of himself Jim shivered.

It was dark now—the moon completely shut out by the flying snow clouds. Small, thin flakes were beginning to come driving up the throat of the cleft. The wind rose continuously.

Jim was aware that there had been no sound of either dogs or wolves for some minutes now. He dashed his hand across his eyes and squinted downcañon through the slanting snow. Nothing was in sight yet. As he stared, the rising storm brought him the renewed noise of the dogs. This time there were not so many voices—no more than five or six, he thought. Before he could attach any significance to this, the battle was rejoined below. It was closer now, not more than half a mile away.

As he listened, a cold chill started from the small of his back and raced up between his shoulder blades. There were no wolf voices in this battle, only the yammering of the dogs. Then even that grew still. The wind died for a few seconds, and the snow seemed to thin. Lewis tightened his fingers on the handle of his stock knife. Trusty friend of many a minor emergency, it was all that stood between him and whatever was coming up the cañon.

And something was coming. Every sense of the trained outdoorsman told him this. He could hear the breathing now, thick and heavy. This was it.

Fifty feet from him the trail shelved sharply downward, cutting off his vision. In front of his prison the cañon floor opened up flaringly to form an almost level-floored arena fifty feet in diameter. He stared across this snow-packed space and waited. The breathing was close now. Just below the rim of the arena there was a crunching and padding of soft footsteps, then, for a moment, no sound at all.

His eyes ached with the strain. He longed to blink but dared not. Finally he had to. When vision cleared, they were there—just above the rim of the arena, on the far side, seeming to float in space, staring straight at him. Four evil soot-black faces, each housing slitted twin yellow coals of

fire—coals that burned searing-hot in the cold belly of the
cañon.

The coup at the entrance of the staircase cleft worked per-
fectly. Wolf-Eye and Sonjii came pounding through the
narrow opening scant inches ahead of the dogs. Five dogs
piled through after them, and the trap was sprung. Barek and
Korok stabbed into the bottleneck of the opening and,
shoulder to shoulder, blocked its thin width. The remaining
dogs piled up outside the trap, howling and leaping madly but
unable to force the situation. Inside the trap the work was
soon done. Rakar and Akhab each killed his dog on the first
rush. Wolf-Eye wheeled and killed one dog and closed with a
second. Crippled Sonjii had a bad moment with his opponent, but bloody Rakar leaped over his own dying victim to
Sonjii's aid. In a few seconds the battle sounds grew still.

Sonjii had taken a severe slash in the flank. The others
were cut up here and there but not seriously. Wolf-Eye, in his
double kill, had taken some severe bites but no crippling
ones. It was a clean victory.

Rakar, wild as usual, was for finishing the rest of the dogs
there and then—charging right out and having done with it
once and for all. Wolf-Eye's deep growl and pointing ears reminded him that they had not yet won clear.

Following the great shepherd's gaze, the three cubs looked
past Barek and Korok, who were still guarding the entrance,
and on down into Icy Meadow. On the far side, still half a
mile away, moved a dark group of figures. In and among the
figures occasional lights flashed and bobbed—men and lan-
terns, humans trailing stubbornly with lights.

Amid the cubs' snarls of confusion Wolf-Eye again gave
the retreat growl. Barek and Korok looked around questioningly. Wolf-Eye repeated the growl. The two gaunt cubs

leaped backward out of the entrance and fled up the cleft after Akhab, Rakar, and Sonjii.

Wolf-Eye dived into the breach and hurled back a presumptuous dog. But immediately he himself was forced to fall back. The hunters were almost across the meadow. Snarling and lunging, he drew away up the cleft, moving backward and facing his circling, eager foes. Overhead the sky went suddenly dark, and he grinned. The moon was gone and that was good, for the outlaw has no better friend than darkness.

XX

"TO THE DEATH"

Rakar took the lead, and Akhab, Barek, and Korok followed unquestioningly. Sonjii limped and staggered in the rear. For a moment the cubs in advance of Sonjii hesitated as though to wait for their injured brother. Rakar snarled threateningly and so led the pack onward up the cleft, ignoring the lagging wounded cub. What use to wait for one who could fight no more? Sonjii was done.

It was the truth. Even as Rakar's last growls were sounding, Sonjii's braced forelegs sagged and buckled. With a retching grunt of pain he slid face downward into the snow and lay still.

Rakar grunted a sharp order, and the remaining cubs turned and fled silently up the cañon. Behind them rose a sudden yelping and baying. The dogs were almost in the second trap. In fact, they *were* in it.

From below came the sudden sounds of fierce battle. At once the fleeing cubs swung about, their four wolfish heads pointed downcañon, their sharp ears pitched intently forward. They sought to catch the sound of their sire's dying snarls, but they sought in vain. Wolf-Eye's famous fighting rumble was not to be heard; only the mad yammering of the hound pack filled the night air. Not a cub moved while the growls and bellowings of the dogs continued. Finally there was silence. It was as though there had never been a hunting dog within fifty miles of Icy Meadow. Not one fragment of telltale sound made its way up the cañon.

At last Akhab's nervous growl broke the eerie stillness. It was over, below. All were dead down there. The sire must lie among the silent ones. Rakar made no attempt to keep the triumph in his snarl hidden.

The wolf dogs turned upcañon without replying to their brother's snarls. They traveled a few minutes in silence, then froze, startled in their tracks. From just above them, upcañon, had come a loud crashing sound as of a heavy body falling. In the confusing wind, which was away from them, it sounded as though the crash and fall had been accompanied by a wild yell. A wild *human* yell!

Rakar, nerves raw with the strain of the past hours, snapped out the silence growl. Absolute quiet was to be had. Barek could not restrain himself. Something was above them in the cañon. The cub's whimper was ragged, frightened. Something was upcañon there. Something had fallen up there—something big, something with a voice like a man.

Akhab growled testily, and Rakar's heavy snarl was contemptuous. Whatever it was, they had to get past it. Man, grizzly, mouse, or mountain, it made no difference. It stood between them and freedom. There was no way around it. Life was dear, and sometimes it had to be bought at the price of death. Whatever was in their way would have to die.

Stepping as gingerly as four giant cats, the gaunt wolf dogs crept upward through the whirling snow. The thing was just above them here—just beyond the rim ahead, where the cleft widened out. They could hear the thing moving about now.

The four flattened to their bellies, slid silently up the last few feet of the trail. Without warning they topped out in a small natural arena. In front of them lay a man, his legs buried in snow and rock débris, his left arm dangling help-lessly, his face and hands covered with blood. He was badly wounded, hopelessly trapped.

Wolf-Eye glanced swiftly behind him. The second ambush, behind which his sons should be waiting, lay a hundred feet away. Now was the time. Putting on a frenzied burst of fighting, he forced his five opponents—all that remained of the dog pack—backward and scattered them. Then, turning, he streaked for the narrow opening behind which his sons would be waiting. By the law of the pack they would be there, waiting for that member that had stayed behind to cover the retreat. The dogs re-gathered and flung themselves after him.

The big shepherd dived through the trap opening with fifty feet to spare. As he whirled to aid his waiting sons in the ambush, his eyes went wide. He was alone! The sons were gone. No—there was Sonjii, down and half hidden in the snow. Wolf-Eye leaped toward him. Where were the cubs? Up, Wise One! What is the matter here?

But there was no sign of life in the battered body. Sonjii's head sagged limply as the dog seized him by the neck ruff. Wolf-Eye dropped him and turned to face the dogs. Raving and howling, they poured through the undefended notch in the trail and bore down on the lone figure crouched in the snow. Fighting tusks bared to the gums, the outlaw dog leaped to meet his civilized brothers. No sound escaped his flaring mouth. This was to the death. There would be no wind to spare for bellowing. With an overwhelming rush the dogs were upon him. He staggered and went down. Half a dozen eager jaws sought his throat.

Sonjii regained consciousness. A few feet upcañon his giant, black-faced sire was battling with his back to the cleft wall. Five fighting dogs hemmed him in.

Sonjii fought for strength. The sire was doomed. He could not chance closing with any one of the dogs for fear the others would smother him the moment he did. All he could do was fight defensively until the hunters from below caught up, but if something should happen to distract the dogs for that split second necessary for the sire to leap among them and kill, then he would be safe. The battered cub summoned every ounce of courage in his fearless heart. Slowly his bloody haunches drew up beneath him. Gradually the blood mist cleared before his eyes. If the dogs could be divided, turned, distracted for just one instant. . . .

Wolf-Eye fought and slashed like a demon, and managed to stay on his feet. But he was trapped. His back was to the cleft wall, and he could move neither right nor left. He dared not rush among the dogs. To close with one would mean to have the other four on his rear immediately. Downcañon the shouts of the hunters drew nearer.

Wolf-Eye gathered himself. He would die, but not beneath a rifle bullet. A split second before he sprang, he checked himself. Up from the snow behind the dogs rose a red-mouthed apparition. With a hoarse roar of challenge it fell upon the rear of the stunned pack. At the same time, Wolf-Eye struck them from the front.

Sonjii's rush split the dogs wide open. He bore one of them down with him as his legs failed in mid-charge. Another dived on his unprotected back. He had broken the back of the first dog with his initial charge, and now he closed his jaws grimly on the throat of the second. Wolf-Eye came to him in a moment. The sounds of battle had ceased miraculously.

Sonjii growled weakly. Wolf-Eye's growl answered him, and the dying cub knew the battle had gone well. One dog dead and two dying for Wolf-Eye, two dead for Sonjii. There were five dogs there in the snow that would never hunt again. Now Wolf-Eye growled at Sonjii, a growl of insistent urging. The dog knew they must go on before the hunters came up. A third time Wolf-Eye gave the whining hurry growl. But it was too late. Sonjii's answering growls were already throaty with the rattle of death. Suddenly they were broken by a violent hemorrhage. When the flow of blood stopped, Sonjii, the fifth, the brave son, was dead.

Wolf-Eye stood a moment over the silent form. From below, the flash of a lantern lit the cañon wall. The men were close. Uttering a deep snarl, the giant dog took the trail of his four traitor sons.

Minutes later he heard a burst of throaty growling from upcañon. Puzzled, he redoubled his speed. Those growls had the sound of the kill in them. The cubs had run into trouble. At the same instant this thought entered the mind of the racing shepherd, a vagrant downdraft from the winds of the upper cleft reversed the air in the cañon for a scant ten seconds. Full and strong to the keen nostrils of the trailing dog came the body scent of a human—*his* human! Rancher Jim Lewis.

From Wolf-Eye's deep lungs burst the killing roar. Harsh and heavy, it thundered up the throat of the staircase cleft. The battle cry of the King of the Mogollons!

XXI

"THE CRY IN THE NIGHT"

For what seemed an eternity the four evil faces stared across at Jim. Then one of them split in a snarl. Deep rumbles from the others followed. Jim watched, fascinated. It sounded as though the brutes were actually talking among themselves.

So these were Wolf-Eye's sons. What brutes! Nearly as large as the dog himself and incredibly more vicious-looking. In spite of himself the rancher thrilled. They were magnificent in their hybrid strength.

Across the arena Rakar snarled at the other cubs. The situation admitted of no indecision. It was a bad spot, and the cruel cub showed his fitness for the leadership in his crisp, hard thinking.

The man in front of them was the one who lived on the banks of Wolf Creek—the one who had killed their dam. The man was the one whose den the sire had shared in his youth. Thus it would be Rakar's pleasure to kill him personally. The man was without the fire weapon that had touched their mother. He was without the ability to harm them. He was badly hurt, as evidenced by the abundance of blood, and he was caught in the rocks and could not even move. Rakar would do the killing now. The others would support him. There was no time to waste. The hunters were coming rapidly from behind them. Wolf-Eye was dead. Rakar was the leader!

As he moved forward, the fearful wolf dogs snarled their approval of Rakar, their savage hatred of the human barring their way to freedom. While they growled and yammered, Jim noticed again how like brutish conversation their snarlings and mouthings were. For all the world, he thought, as if they were arranging it among them how they were going to do him in. Man-like, he would never have believed how near truth his thoughts were.

Across from him, now, the four great animals came forward as one, their cold eyes glued on the helpless rancher. With death less than fifty feet from him, Jim found time to marvel at the unreality of the whole situation. Less than half a mile away were a dozen men with rifles. He could hear them coming, for the wind was his way. He thought of screaming for help. No use, though. The wind would kill the sounds within a hundred yards. Those devils were going to murder him, and twenty minutes later his neighbors and the professional hunters would be standing at the scene, and old Clay Peters would be muttering: "In forty years I've never knowed a wolf to kill a man."

He watched the wolf dogs coming. Wolf-Eye's sons. They were going to kill him. The dog was dead, and his sons were going to kill his old master. Jim remembered the heavy voice of old August Helm, warning him that the dog carried the "stamp of the wolf." Jim could hear his own confident laugh, then, and the words that had followed. Gosh, that had been a long time ago! He had had his way and taken the puppy, but the old man had been right. Wolf-Eye's blood was coming out. And it was going to cost a human life in the process. The man who had once saved the gray shepherd puppy's life was about to die for doing so. Things sure worked out funny. What was the saying about "biting the hand that fed you"? Old Wolf-Eye was sure paying him back in a bad way.

Yet he felt no hatred of the big dog—far from it. He was sorry for him! Here he was, about to be done for by the dog's own offspring, and he was feeling sorry for the dog! It was a funny world.

The rushing cub brutes were almost on top of him. Still his last thoughts were of Wolf-Eye. At the last split instant he could think of nothing but the dog. For no reason in the world he opened his mouth and yelled into the faces of the leaping wolf dogs.

"Hi . . . Wolf-Eye!"

It was the old work call he had used to put the big shepherd dog on cattle. As he yelled it now, it appeared to him, for the moment, as though his reason had snapped. For he imagined he saw the great dog suddenly appear in answer to his wild call. He threw his broken arm across his throat and fell forward to protect his face and eyes from the attacking cubs. His right hand drew back, clenching the stock knife. He felt the weight of the first attacker on his shoulders and struck blindly upward with the knife.

Wolf-Eye, galloping madly toward the sound of the cubs' snarling, burst over the rim of the arena and halfway across it before his eyes caught up with his speed. Rakar, Akhab, Barek, and Korok were upon his master. Trapped and half buried in the rock and snow, the man lay helpless beneath their furious charge. In his hand he clutched a short knife and from his lips burst a single defiant yell.

"Hi . . . Wolf-Eye!"

Then the cubs were upon him. With a bellow of insane rage the giant shepherd dog charged.

XXII

"WOLF-EYE'S ANSWER"

Wolf-Eye appeared among them and fought in utter silence and with the fury of a dozen rabid wolves. The cubs, confronted by a ghost dog who fought with real teeth and jaws and panicky with suddenness of the onslaught, fought back with the bursting frenzy of the cornered wild animal. Rakar went berserk. Akhab and Barek followed him blindly. Korok would never follow any wolf again. He lay retching out his life in the snow, dead in the first charge from a broken neck and ripped throat. Gone, now, was all thought of the human. Jim had not even been scratched, so furious and devastating had been Wolf-Eye's arrival among the cubs. The rancher watched now, awe-stricken.

The action moved in blinding whirls and blurs of gray and black and red fur. Fangs slashed, red mouths gaped, yellow eyes blazed. The air shook with the impact and thudding of the powerful bodies, and with the sound of the wolf dogs' crazed bellowings.

Jim had not seen Wolf-Eye for a year and a half. The change in the great dog was amazing. Except for his black face he was more wolf-like than his sons. He was the range killer personified. Jim shivered as he watched the huge dog.

Jaws raving, yellow eyes smoky-red with battle fire, great muscles writhing and leaping, the gray shepherd fought the battle of ten thousand years of heritage. With death on the

131

scales and the life of his master in the balance, he fought the only fight a dog can fight—the fight of faith in a man.

Akhab was down now, his abdomen sliced open from rib basket to groin, but his killing had given Rakar and Barek an instant's opening. They were closing before Wolf-Eye could recover from delivering Akhab's deathblow. The dog braced himself for the shock. It came with a rush. Less weakened by wounds than their sire and having the advantage of the attack, the two cubs bore him raving to the ground. Barek's mighty jaws closed on his great thigh and ground harshly into the living bone. At the same time Rakar was at his throat.

With a swift upward lunge Wolf-Eye met Rakar's thrust. Fang ground into fang, and the traitorous cub drew back, screaming in wounded rage. The right side of his face was laid open to the bone. In this brief instant Wolf-Eye writhed out from under Rakar and threw himself, twisting, onto Barek. His raking fangs struck the latter on the shoulder and opened his side backward and downward across the rib cage. Strangling with pain, Barek let go his hold of Wolf-Eye's thigh and rolled clear. The blood-covered shepherd whirled just in time to receive Rakar's return charge. In so doing he stumbled over the still thrashing and screaming Barek. Again the three were down in a heap.

Under the mass of the two surging bodies, Wolf-Eye's mind grew hazy. Blood filled his eyes. He felt fangs on his shoulder searching for his throat. A great weight lay across his rear legs. He could not move.

"Wolfie! Wolfie, boy!" The cry came again, the man's voice beating through the dog's failing senses. "Hi . . . Wolf-Eye!"

The strength flowed from somewhere. The dog's will responded to the man's. The necessity to obey when the command came, the automatic reflex of performing long-

forgotten tasks on demand, and above all the thrilling sound
of his master calling again to him in the old wonderful voice
of their working days came hammering into Wolf-Eye's
brain. The great dog was up again. Rakar rolled clear of the
struggle, but Barek lunged, half falling across his rear, seizing
Wolf-Eye in the loins. The huge jaw muscles writhed spasmodically. There was a final clamping crunch, and Barek was
free—to join his ancestors.

For a moment Wolf-Eye and Rakar faced each other. Jim
watched spellbound. Tears filled his eyes, and his stomach
felt sick and empty. The whole brutal action had taken only
seconds, yet the dog hadn't so much as glanced at the man.
Still, the rancher knew he was watching the last act of one of
the strangest plays of faith ever performed. Wolf-Eye, renegade, outlaw, fabled killer, was living out his final hour in the
tradition of his breed—in service to mankind. He was dying a
dog. He was ready now to make the last payment on his debt
to humanity. That it was long overdue could be forgotten;
that he was making it at all would be remembered.

Rakar moved confidently. He was stronger than his sire.
The latter's right rear leg was shattered to the bone. His
shoulder was laid bare. A dozen long wounds scarred his
haunches, back, and sides. He had lost a great deal of blood.
Rakar himself was many times wounded, but only superfi-
cially. His strength and fighting skill remained virtually un-
damaged. His hate was stronger than ever. He was arrogantly
superior, snarling, disdainful of his mortally wounded sire.
He prepared to attack.

Wolf-Eye, so weak he scarcely could stand but scorning
Rakar to the last, attacked first. It was a surprise move and
caught the cruel cub flat-footed. The two rolled over and
over. Wolf-Eye knew he could never regain his feet, knew his
strength was gone. He had gambled everything on this one

abrupt and unorthodox charge. And he won.

As the two survivors rolled, locked in the death struggle, the shepherd's wide jaws were closed like steel traps on Rakar's chest just below the throat juncture. Rakar thrashed and fought like a fiend. The shepherd's jaws worked methodically, grinding and chewing relentlessly upward toward the jugular. Rakar's wild slashing slowed—faltered—ceased suddenly. His body lashed in one final convulsion.

For a moment there was no other movement. Then Wolf-Eye swung his great head aloft, freeing his jaws from Rakar's throat.

His voice thick with tears, Jim called softly to him. "Hi . . . Wolf-Eye!" Then shamelessly, tears coursing down the bronze seams of his face, he sobbed aloud. "Oh, Wolfie! Wolfie, boy!"

With an effort the dog pulled himself from the beneath the dead body of Rakar, the traitor. With agonizing slowness he dragged himself across the blood-soaked snow. It took him ten minutes to make the journey from the battlefield to his master's hand—a distance of fifteen feet.

All the while Jim spoke to him gently, encouragingly. At last he came to the big man's side. One final effort and he collapsed, his head in the crook of his master's arm, his torn shoulder pressed against the rancher's chest. He was quiet then for several seconds. Jim made no sound. His powerful arm held the great dog close. Wolf-Eye's yellow eyes opened, turned sheepishly upward to gaze into his master's face. His plumed tail swept the snow in slow, graceful circles. He lifted his head, then tucked it with shy diffidence against his deep-furred chest. Wolf-Eye, the killer King of the Mogollons, was embarrassed. It was for all the world as though he expected to be told in a stern voice, of course, that he was a bad dog!

Jim couldn't repress a smile, although it came through unabashed tears. "Wolfie," he managed, his arm pressing the dog's torn head to his cheek, "you big damned fool, you."

The tail moved once more, weakly. The great black face wrinkled. The pink tongue quickly flicked out along the tear-stained brown cheek. The steady yellow eyes moved once more shyly upward, then closed slowly. A deep, grateful sigh relaxed the tired body. The great, heavy head burrowed a moment in the crook of the protecting arm, then rested quietly. Jim felt the fierce heart beat wildly against his, then grow still.

The wind seemed to have slackened. The rancher raised his head. The snow clouds were banking back upon themselves. The moon rode clear and bright in the open sky. Downcañon, lights and voices were approaching. Old Clay Peters's voice was grumbling.

"It beats all what become of them varmints. We ain't heard a sound out of them in twenty minutes now. Wonder what all the infernal racket was up here, anyway."

The first of the men topped the rise and came into the far side of the arena.

"Over here, boys," called Jim.

The men stopped and stared intently.

"Who's that?" one of them demanded.

"It's me, boys," the rancher answered wearily. "Jim Lewis."

"Holy smokes! It *is* Jim," breathed a young rancher, holding his lantern high, as the others crowded forward around the injured man. "And it sure enough looks like he's found his dog at last."

There was a pause then, till the drawling voice of Clay Peters broke the stillness.

"Reckon you've got that just about backward, son." As the

135

old man spoke, his range-wise eyes drifted slowly around the moonlit scene of destruction. " 'Pears to me like the dog finally found Jim!"

Again there was silence as all eyes turned to Jim. The men, feeling somehow that the real answer was yet to come, waited for him to speak. After a long moment he did.

"You're both wrong, boys." The big Wolf Creek ranchman's words came soft and thoughtful, as though the mind that framed them was traveling slowly and far away. "Wolf-Eye finally found himself."

The Legend of Trooper Hennepin

The day had been another bad one for the cavalry. A small patrol had been ambushed north of Doña Ana with three men killed. A strong detachment had caught the raiders at the Mexican settlement of San Miguel and shot five Apaches in retaliation. Major Sanford Ash, commanding the troops based at Mesilla, understood that he was confronted with a most serious situation. Since sundown, he had been closeted with his senior civilian scout in a last effort to come up with some useful, meaningful action short of the Indian war so plainly threatened in his area.

Leaving that meeting, now, the scout went quickly through the night toward B barracks. His thoughts were already far from Mesilla, and, when presently he found young Trooper Hennepin stretched out on a bench in front of the barracks, his words hurried to catch up with those thoughts.

"Hennepin, I just got you a thirty-day leave. That is, providing you want to spend it with me hunting Apaches. Or have you lost your taste for Mescalero meat?"

"Mister Peckinpaugh," said the red-headed youth, "please don't prod me. You know how bad I feel about Soldado's bunch getting away from us down to San Miguel this afternoon."

"I reckon I do. You was interested in my girl, Pilar, wasn't you?"

"Yes, sir. But, damn it, Mister Peckinpaugh, them crazy Mexicans in the town didn't tell us the Apaches had grabbed her until we got back from chasing them down past old Fort Fillmore. Them Mexes are all yellow dogs, blast their souls."

"No, they ain't, Red." The white-bearded scout used Hennepin's nickname affectionately, quietly, as though the boy were his own son. "They got to live with the Apaches after the U.S. cavalry has come and gone. It's a heap different for them. And remember, I know them well. Pilar's mother was a Mexican."

"Yes, but Pilar. . . ."

"Forget it, boy." The old man cut him off abruptly. "Your detachment done what it could. Pilar's gone, that's the fact. Next fact is we still got our jobs to do, which is why I asked the major to spare you for a spell. I can use a pair of young eyes out there, Red."

Trooper Hennepin was bone weary. He had been out scouting with old Ben Peckinpaugh before. Born in the horse Indian country across the Pecos, the young cavalryman was a good tracker, fluent in the sign language, did not suffer from the Indian nerves that afflicted so many of his fellow troopers. But a few trips with Peckinpaugh were enough for a lifetime. The old man was a terror, more Apache than most Apaches in his energies and attitudes. To spend thirty days with him in a general search for the red brother was hardly the stuff of a young cavalryman's favorite dreams.

"Well, no, thanks, Mister Peckinpaugh." He tried to make the refusal reasonable. "Why don't you take Beecher, or One-Ear McGonigle? They're good scouts. Or get that Lipan Apache, Cuddles. He's the best in the regiment."

"I got better use for you, Red. Major Ash wants us to bring

in the Apache who's bossing this trouble. He says to find him, whoever he is, and fetch him back to talk peace."

"I can't see it, Mister Peckinpaugh. You know there's only one Apache I'd be interested in going after."

"I reckon that's why I'm here, boy."

Hennepin stiffened. "You think Soldado's the chief that's been stirring up the Mescaleros?"

"That's the name I guessed at for Major Ash. You know a Mescalero chief needs a dose of peace talk any worse?"

"So that's it!" said Hennepin. "You come looking for me, figuring I'd be a cinch to say yes on account of Pilar?"

Ben Peckinpaugh nodded. "You telling me I figured wrong?"

Trooper Hennepin stood up, all six feet and four inches of him. "No, sir," he said. "Hang on, I'll get my gun."

"Good idea," said the cynical scout. "Soldado may remember you from this afternoon. Cuddles tells me you cracked his skull with a long shot across the river . . . knocked him kicking off his pony. Two braves had to scoop him up and carry him off between their horses. That right?"

"Yes, sir. It was a lucky shot."

Peckinpaugh stared at the young trooper. He shifted his quid of Brown's Mule and spat acridly.

"Red," he said, "you got an awful lot to learn about Apache luck."

Hennepin's bay had been eating oats from a nosebag. He was full of go. Even Old Roan, Peckinpaugh's bony gelding, was showing a little ginger. As the two scouts mounted up and started away from the picket line, a third familiar horse came out of the night—Cuddles's miserable Indian black.

"Me go 'long by you," the little Lipan Apache told Peckinpaugh. "Me decide you grow too old. You no smell

Injun good like in old days."

"You go to blazes!" growled Peckinpaugh, but Hennepin could sense what he meant was more like: "Glad to see you, you red runt. Lead on. We're right behind you."

They went that night only as far as Dripping Springs, a water hole on the Apache trail to San Augustine Pass. Cuddles herded them into some boulders above the springs and said: "We wait here. Guide come by and by. Keep pony quiet."

Before long, a cactus owl hooted three times from the desert to the east and, when Cuddles had hooted back, floated in without noise to join them in the rocks. It proved to be a very paunchy owl with a Spanish accent and a Comanche profile.

"Him Gomez, the Comanchero," said Cuddles. "Him know way."

"Buenas noches, patrónes." Gomez nodded to the two scouts. "You are in good time. Let us keep it that way."

"Like you said, Mister Peckinpaugh," admitted Hennepin admiringly, as they set out, "we got our jobs to do. It surely does help, though, to know the arrangements has all been took care of so thorough."

"Yup. See you remember it. It saves hair."

They rode at a steady gait until shortly before dawn, when Gomez brought them to a hidden *tinaja,* or pothole water tank, on the far side of the Organ and San Andres mountains. That next night, and the nights following it, they rode northeast across the great dry Tularosa Sink, past the weird and lifeless gypsum drifts of the White Sands, to Alamogordo at the foot of the Sacramento range. Here, they turned due north toward the town of Tularosa, then hard east to Bent's Mill, and again northeast, past Ruidoso, into the timber-dark jumble of the Jicarilla and Capitán mountains, so coming at last to the granite-guarded homeland of the Mescalero Apaches. Here, Gomez left them, saying no farewells.

"You could smell the fear in his sweat," said Peckinpaugh.

To which Cuddles nodded quickly. "Sure, him no damn' fool like us."

Trooper Hennepin said nothing. He found his tongue only after he and Peckinpaugh had given their horses over to Cuddles to take back and hide out on the trail "so even him new sun no see when him come up." "Lordy!" said the young soldier to his white-bearded companion. "This is spooky. Where in the world are we?"

The veteran scout waved carelessly. "Well, Red, getting off them ponies just now, we'd ought to be about one hundred crow-flight miles out of Mesilla, and eight thousand foot up on the north shoulder of Sierra Blanca peak. Come daybreak and, according to the priceless trail instructions furnished us by the vanishing *Señor* Gomez, we'd ought to be staring straight into the secret mountain *ranchería* of our Mescalero friend, Soldado."

In the blackness before dawn, Hennepin's tired mind marched all the way to Peckinpaugh's small ranch outside San Miguel. From there, his thoughts went to the cavalry encampment near Mesilla and back again, to where he shivered on the chill heights of Sierra Blanca above Soldado's *ranchería*. In all the long journey, only Pilar Peckinpaugh's luminous face burned with any lasting brightness. He had thought of little else save the slim girl since learning the Apache had taken her. Now the feeling of her possible nearness was very strong. He would have thought that sleep would be as far from him as the coldest star in this circumstance, yet drowse he did. Peckinpaugh's voice touched him on the shoulder.

"Sorry, Red. But we're close now. Got to stay awake forty-eight hours a day. You were dreaming, wide-eyed."

"I know, Mister Peckinpaugh. I won't do it again. I was thinking about your girl."

"Sure, boy, so was I."

Again the silence grew deep. Down on the mountain the quail were beginning to call. Over east, 'way over east, the rim of the prairie world was turning pale.

"Mister Peckinpaugh . . . ?"

"Yup."

"You think we'll find Pilar?"

"I hope so."

"You reckon she'll be all right, providing we do?"

"It ain't hardly likely. They've had her too long."

This time, when the silence settled in, it stayed a longer while. Finally there was only the morning star remaining on the horizon. Hennepin shivered and said: "Mister Peckinpaugh, how's your Comanche twitch doing?"

The bearded scout shook his head. "Well, the itch has been on me since sundown, Red. That means they're powerful close, you know."

"Yes, sir. But the nose twitch . . . it ain't set in on you yet, eh?" Hennepin anxiously named the last in the sequence of symptoms in his companion's renowned ability to *smell* the nearness of the Apache enemy.

"Funny thing," said Peckinpaugh. "It just started twitching."

Hennepin felt his stomach shrink. "Where's Cuddles?" he asked. "I ain't seen him since he took the horses off."

"Neither have I. Likely he just kept going with the horses. We're afoot, boy. And far from home."

The eerie stillness of the mountain daybreak seemed all at once magnified. The quail stopped calling on the slope below. The rosy flush of the sun was tipping the Capitáns. Hennepin's voice sounded unnaturally loud to him.

"Maybe we'd ought to have gone with Cuddles. It feels to me as though we might have got a little too close to Soldado's *ranchería* without asking his consent. What you think, Mister Peckinpaugh?"

It was not the old scout who answered, but a deep young voice from the mountainside above and behind them.

"Yes, Mister Peckinpaugh, what do you think?"

The English was very good, and there seemed no anger in the fine bass voice, but the old man shrank visibly.

"Don't move!" he hissed at Hennepin. "That's Soldado."

"That's right," said the Apache chief. "Turn around without your guns."

They stood up slowly, hands elevated slightly.

Their turn to face the Mescalero had all the restrained grace of two figures suspended in heavy syrup. When they had completed it, old Ben Peckinpaugh looked at the pack of Apache riflemen standing on the rocks above and said regretfully to Trooper Hennepin: "Red, we're gone up."

And Trooper Hennepin, just as regretfully, acknowledged: "Mister Peckinpaugh, that's so."

With that, they waited for the crash of the Indian rifles.

It did not come.

Instead, Soldado raised his right hand and spoke to Hennepin. "I won't shoot you as you did me, *schichobe*," he said gravely to the young trooper. "I've been waiting for you."

"Watch it!" warned Peckinpaugh. "Either Soldado's being funny, which no Apache never ain't, or he's actually tooken a shine to you. Treat him gentle, whichever. He just called you old friend."

The *ranchería* lay in a tiny deep valley of incrdeible beauty.

The Mescaleros, skillfully employing the creek that plunged down off Sierra Blanca, had irrigated corn and melons. Their mud-and-cedar dwellings, the typical beehive *jacales* of the Apaches, were neatly kept, stoutly made. The women and children and old ones who stared at the white captives as they were brought down off the mountain, were well-dressed, handsome savages. The pony herds grazing the flower-dotted grasses along the creek were of high quality. Goat, sheep, and even a few cattle fed quietly in the farther meadows. Trooper Hennepin, who had never seen a wild Apache *ranchería,* was astonished at the obvious social order and intelligence among Soldado's people, and this was overlain by his awe at the natural splendors of the place wherein they dwelled. "Jings," he said softly aloud to Peckinpaugh, "this place ain't possible!"

The old man only nodded. He looked past the tall youth at the mountain walls that would form their prison or their tomb. It was in truth a striking, impossible place: a high, lost valley, full of solitude and frightening silence, yet a green jewel of lush grass, aspen, birch, pine, cedar, bending willow, and seedling mountain grape, all set in a ring of platinum water, harsh red rock, and raw blue sky. The impact of it left a man humble and dumb, left him shaking his head and thinking inside himself, even as Hennepin was thinking: *Dear Lord above, how beautiful it is!*

Peckinpaugh had been in other places such as this one; their lure had driven him to forty years of nomad wandering. Each time he thought: *Next time I shall stay and seek no more. I shall have found my trail's end and shall wander no farther. I shall have found my* querencia, *and I shall remain within its blessed shelter forever.*

Yet in forty years Peckinpaugh had not found his *querencia,* his place of last retreat and security, and now, suddenly, he knew he never would find it, that, indeed, it had never existed outside his restless heart. And he saw, in the strange way young Trooper Hennepin was looking at this valley of impossible beauty, the same yearnings he himself had followed all the wasted years. It was a peculiar moment for such a thought and the stern resolve it fathered—being marched as he and Hennepin were into a life or death of Apache cruelty—but Ben Peckinpaugh determined in that moment that the red-headed boy should not suffer the heartache he had suffered, and that had destroyed his own chance for a real home and lasting happiness. Come what may, Hennepin must be gotten out of the valley before its wild call lured him away from his own people, as another valley beneath another mountain in another time had lured Ben Peckinpaugh.

The summer days became weeks. The Mescalero autumn songs and corn dance prayers were intoned. The sunlit hours, yet golden with warmth, became shorter. The high air sharpened with the frosts of coming winter. Still the white scouts languished in captivity, still they listened to the dance chants, and wondered when the rhythms would change to those of the *Dah-eh-sah,* Dance of the Dead, signaling their end.

But the drums did not summon them. Their strange imprisonment endured unbroken. By night they slept in the *jacal* of To-klani, Soldado's elder statesman and adviser. By day they went to shuck and grind corn, women's work, or to help in the horse breaking and branding, the labor of men, or were put to digging new irrigation ditches, the menial indignity of slaves. Always and wherever they went, they went in company with their guards: Puercito, Little Pig, and Carnicero, Butcher. They were not bound during the day, but they understood the Apache terms of this freedom. If they broke to flee, Little Pig and Butcher would shoot them. Little

Pig and Butcher would do this because, if they did not, *they* would be shot, a simple arrangement guaranteeing at once the docility of the prisoners and the alertness of the guards.

At each day's end, To-klani padlocked them with ancient Spanish slave collars to the wall of his *jacal*. When he did this, he would shrug and say without rancor: "At the least sound of the chains being worked with, I shall shoot you both through the middle of your bellies."

Beyond these fundamental restraints there was one social stricture: they were permitted no contact whatever with the Apache women. Hennepin reasoned this was because their captors feared the white men would work on the women to aid them in escape. To this nonsense Peckinpaugh snorted disdainfully.

"Huh, it's to keep the women from working on us, Red, and not to let us escape!"

Hearing this remark, Little Pig said in a friendly fashion: "Old Horse is right, Red Hair. Listen to him. I would prefer the mercies of Butcher to those of our women. *Ay de mí!*"

Yet the young trooper could not put the women from his mind. Would they not be the ones who would know of Pilar? The men certainly did not—or would not admit they did. His and Peckinpaugh's repeated attempts to question Little Pig and Butcher, even old To-klani, as to the girl's well-being and whereabouts drew only blank stares or Apache shrugs. Finally, two days before this, Butcher had struck Hennepin across the face with his rifle butt and rasped in Spanish: "*¡Collate!* I am sick of hearing about the cursed girl. Ask me one more time, now, and I will shoot you." He had added the Apache qualification—"*zas-tee!*"—and asked if Hennepin understood the term. The red-headed trooper had nodded that his growing Mescalero vocabulary did include the word *zas-tee*—kill—that he was grateful to Butcher for the reminder in the mouth, just then, and that he would remember him for it.

About one thing, at last, they were able to gain information. This was the matter of the long delay in judging their case. It seemed, according to Little Pig, that there was a fundamental split in tribal policy over the white captives. Kahtanay, a warrior of considerable influence and a hater of the white man, headed one faction, Soldado, the other. The young chief held that Old Horse Peckinpaugh and the boy soldier Red Hair were telling the truth about their mission to find Soldado and ask him to come in for a peace talk at Mesilla. Kahtanay called Soldado a foolish boy himself, scarcely older than Red Hair and, moreover, crazy to trust the white scouts. The two *gringos* would never have come down off Sierra Blanca except as captives, and the entire purpose of their presence upon the mountain had been to spy on the *rancheria* so that they might return to Mesilla and lead the Pony Soldiers down upon Soldado's people and destroy them. There was only one safe, sensible thing to do with those white men: *zas-tee*.

The whole problem, Little Pig told them on this third day following Butcher's attack on Hennepin, was going to be voted on that same afternoon. The members of the council would put either a long stick or a short stick into a big tobacco bowl. The long stick meant freedom for the white captives; the short stick—well, what was the difference, really? Did not all of Yosen's creatures sooner or later arrive at the identical end? But of course, it was only natural.

It was well after dark when Soldado sent for Hennepin to be brought to his *jacal*. In the light from the lamb's fat candles, the Apache youth appeared more savagely handsome than before. Hennepin's gesture of respect toward him, a touch of the finger tips to the brow, was spontaneous

The young chief returned the sign with quiet dignity, murmuring in Spanish: "We are much alike, my brother. Sit here with me." Studying the red-headed trooper a moment, he added: "Perhaps you do not feel this as I do?"

"Do you mean the likeness?" said Hennepin, also in Spanish. "If so, yes, I have felt it. I thought from the first moment that we were friends. But since that time I have wondered what manner of friends."

Soldado nodded. An oddly sad expression softened his dark features. "I have treated you as I have because it was necessary for your own safety. This is why I had you brought here tonight. I wished you to hear some things about me and my people before I told you how the council vote went for you and for Old Horse Peckinpaugh this afternoon."

He paused, looking at his guest. Hennepin tried to imagine what thoughts passed behind that Indian mask, but he knew enough of Soldado's kind to realize he could never guess.

"I will tell you my story, now," the Apache youth concluded softly. "Listen well, Red Hair, for I want you to understand. . . ."

Soldado was a troubled red man. The son and grandson of chiefs, he said, he had come to his position as headman of the Sierra Blanca band by heredity among a people who did not believe that tribal power should be passed down by blood. Among the Apaches, any man could be chief, and the Apache preferred that any man could be chief. The unfortunate truth was that Soldado's people were fanatics about personal liberty. To them, individual freedom was a religion. With every man, woman, and child in the Apache country doing precisely what he or she wished, and nothing whatever which might be wished upon them by some other, wiser person, the result was chaos. It was the entire weakness of the red man in his war against the white man.

Young Soldado's cross was that it had been given to him by his father to manage this weakness of the Apache people. The old man had charged his son to use his life to protect his kinsmen from their disease of unbridled self-will. "Remember always," the dying chief had told Soldado, "that to buy a little freedom, much freedom must be spent." Teach that fact to their people, he had said, and, if they would not accept the lesson sensibly, then beat it into them with a rifle butt. If stronger instructions were called for, there was always the other end of the rifle.

So far, Soldado had used neither butt nor barrel of the rifle, but in this second year of his leadership big trouble had come upon his people. The hotheads and cultists of the ancient Apache *Hesh-Ke* sect—a secret brotherhood founded on the meaning of its name, "a rage to kill"—had commenced to raid the white settlements along the Río Grande. Kahtanay and part of Soldado's Sierra Blanca band had been among the guilty in these affairs, against Soldado's express wishes.

Now, Soldado was no friend of the white man's. His father's advice had not included any instruction that he should attempt to cultivate the white brother. "Only avoid him as the wolf avoids the poisoned bait," the old chief had said. "Circle wide around him when you see him. If you do not see him and are forced into a fight with him, then kill all that you can of him. And if you can kill all of him, kill *all*. For if one white man is left alive to bear the tale, a hundred will come back in his place, and our people will be killed again and again, until there are no more of them left alive in this land."

Soldado did not claim innocence of blame in the present Mesilla Valley trouble. As chief of the Sierra Blanca Mescaleros the responsibility was his, and he accepted it. But he was not personally a *Hesh-Ke,* not personally the hater and killer of the white man that the white man said he was. He did not blame the white men for thinking this of him. He only denied that it was true. Soldado had killed, yes, and would kill again. The white man would not have it any other way. He hated the Apaches, and the Apaches did not love him. It had been so from the first, except for the brief time of Cochise. Now that time was over, and Kahtanay and his *Hesh-Ke* kind were in power: there would be a war, now, and no white man could stop it and few Indians would want to.

War was in the autumn air. The excitement of it was too strong in the Apache nostrils to be expelled. The Pony Soldiers made a great mistake in trying to talk peace and to be brothers with the Apaches. Kahtanay and the *Hesh-Ke* took this for a sign of weakness. Soldado, of course, knew better than this. He, for one, was sorry about the Doña Ana and San Miguel treacheries. True, Kahtanay had led those raiding parties, and Soldado had gone down into the valley only to bring the raiders back, to call them away from their murderous work. That was why Soldado had been seen at the San Miguel fight. But who would ever believe his story?

And, indeed, what white man should believe it?

It was the entire tragedy of the Indian way. While one chief made peace, his brother chief was making war. While Soldado might be shaking hands with the enemy at Mesilla, Kahtanay was killing the enemy at Doña Ana. This wildness was not the white man's fault. It was the Indian's. But until the white man could understand the Indian's way, there could never be real peace, or even any useful talk of a real peace. The Pony Soldiers could not continue to kill the good people of one Apache chief for what the bad people of another Apache chief had done. When one white man murdered another white man, did the Pony Soldiers ride out and shoot down five strange white men who had never even heard of the other two white men?

"No, my brother," Soldado concluded, placing his hand on Hennepin's shoulder. "Until your people stop killing mine simply because they are Apaches, there can be no peace between us. I tell you this carefully, Red Hair, because of what I must say." He fell silent, then, plainly not wanting to continue.

Hennepin touched him hesitantly upon the arm. "Before you tell me," he said, "may I ask you something? Why do you call me friend and brother? We speak of a mutual liking, but actually we have something more than the colors of our skin separating our hearts. Do you know of what I speak?"

Soldado nodded. "You mean the girl, Pilar."

"Yes. What of her?"

"I did not take her. Kahtanay already had seized her and gone on when I rode into San Miguel and you caught me there with your Pony Soldiers and gave me this wound in the head." He touched the bandage above his ears, dark smile flashing ruefully. "Kahtanay was back here at our *rancheria* before me, and all that I could do was try to protect Old Horse's daughter. I could not set her free for reasons of Apache law."

"And that is it?"

"No. After that, I lost my heart to Pilar."

"*Oh,*" said Hennepin very quietly. "Thank you, Soldado."

The young chief did not reply at once but rather studied his companion closely. It was the Apache way. Unlike the white brother, the Indian had the habit of thinking before he talked. That was because what he said was important to him. His words were not just pebbles in the mouth to be spat out so that the tongue might be more comfortable, or given greater room to wag.

"In our lives," he said at last, and slowly, "we meet many men. Their numbers are as the leaves of the aspen. And, as the leaves of the aspen, they talk too much and say too little. You and I have not said three score words before tonight. But in the first moment on the mountain our eyes spoke for us, and they said . . . 'We are friends. Our hearts are good for one another. We are happy to see each other.' Do you agree, Red Hair?"

"Yes," said Hennepin. "I was thrilled to see you there. I felt only pride when you called me *friend*."

"Only pride? Nothing else?"

"Yes, I felt something else. But I can't describe it."

"I can," said Soldado. "Among all of those we meet upon the long trail of life, only a few, no more than the fingers of a man's hand, do we remember as friends . . . real friends." The Apache youth held up his right hand. "Here is my hand, Red Hair. I count you first among its fingers."

Before Hennepin could think to reply to this testament, Soldado offered the hand to his white companion.

"From this night when our hands meet," he said, "we are true brothers."

The young trooper returned Soldado's grip fervently. Then embarrassment overcame both of them. Soldado pulled away his hand with some awkwardness.

"Now," he said, "I must tell you how the vote went."

"Thank you," Hennepin nodded.

He was certain he already knew how the vote had gone. No doubt he and Peckinpaugh were to be banished down the mountain, their peace mission for the Pony Soldiers a failure. For an Apache, such a failure would be great punishment. So Hennepin reasoned. It followed that Soldado should look worried now, since, of course, he would not want to injure the pride of his brother.

"Please do not fret over it," he said to the Apache chief. "I understand that you have no choice but to do as the council voted should be done. I am ready."

"Good," said Soldado. "I am glad to hear that. It is true I have no choice. Among my people, where the fate of the entire band may be involved, the vote of the headmen in council is final. It eases my mind that you know about this."

"It is nothing, my brother," said Hennepin graciously. "How did the vote go?"

Soldado looked at him, fierce eyes gleaming in the candle-light. "It went poorly," he said, his voice low. "You and Old Horse will be shot in the morning when the sun strikes the top peak of the Capitáns."

Butcher pushed Hennepin with his boot sole, sending him sprawling through the low door of To-klani's *jacal.* "Lock him up!" he snapped at the Apache elder. "And you better sleep lightly tonight. If anything happens to these prisoners, Kahtanay will cut your liver out. He told me to tell you that."

"Kahtanay will do well to worry about his own liver," said To-klani quietly. "Get away from my house, war talker."

"When Kahtanay is chief," sneered the other, "I will remind him of your great friendship."

"Do that." To-klani nodded. "But now get out of my doorway. The wind is from your direction, and the stink it bears is like that from a sick dog."

"That will be remembered, also, when Kahtanay is chief!"

"I fear your yapping like I fear the bark of *enh,* the fierce prairie dog," said the old man. He picked up his rifle. "I am cocking my rifle, as you will see. That is because I intend to fire a shot with it through that doorway where you stand."

Butcher cursed and leaped aside. The bullet from To-klani's stolen Pony Soldier carbine splintered the door branch on the side of his exit. A string of Apache profanity was heard, outside, then departing footsteps.

"The bullet," said To-klani, "speaks in a tongue all men understand."

"A true thing," agreed Peckinpaugh. "What do you think, *anciano?* Will the young chief shoot us, or not? How went the vote of the headmen?"

"I don't know. Go to sleep."

"I know," said Hennepin, gulping audibly. "Soldado just told me. We'll be shot at sunrise."

"He'll never do it, Red. Not Soldado."

To-klani shook his head. "If the council voted against you, you will be shot. Soldado did not lie when he said it. Now be quiet, both of you. I'm old. I need my sleep."

"One favor," said Peckinpaugh. "Let me ask Red Hair what Soldado told him about my daughter, Pilar."

"I have no daughter, but I can understand how you feel. Go ahead."

The old scout wheeled excitedly on Hennepin. "Well?" he demanded. "What did Soldado tell you. Where is she? Is she well? Have they harmed her? What have the devils done with her?"

"Lordy!" blurted Hennepin, amazed at himself. "I don't know. I plumb forgot to ask."

"You *what?*"

"I was so bowled over by Soldado telling me he was going to have us shot in the morning, I plain forgot to ask about Pilar . . . I mean about where she is, and all."

Peckinpaugh sagged down in his iron dog collar, speechless.

"Mister Peckinpaugh," muttered Hennepin, "I'm just as sorry as a man can be."

"Never mind, Red." The old man's words were weary, beaten, forlorn. "You'd ought to have asked, though. The least thing you could have did, boy, was to find out about my girl. It would have helped me a mortal lot to stand up to those devils in the morning to know that Pilar was alive and all right."

Before Hennepin could reply to what little Soldado *had* told him of the girl, a tall shadow loomed in the doorway, and the young chief's deep voice startled them all.

"I will tell you about the girl, Old Horse," he said. "I meant to tell Red Hair, and I forgot." He hesitated, and they could see it was not an easy thing for him. "I love your daughter, but a proud man will not take by force what he cannot gain by consent. Your daughter loves another. She is well, and no man has touched her." He turned to Hennepin. "I must tell you now a thing that twists in me as a rusted lance blade, Red Hair . . . you are that other one Pilar loves."

As silently as he had come, Soldado was gone.

Hennepin and Peckinpaugh sat in their chains staring at one another, searching for something to say. Presently the old scout muttered: "You were dead right about that Indian, Red. He's a stray for certain."

"Shut up!" gritted To-klani. "Love, pride, women, bah! Shut up and let an old man get some sleep!" He turned his face to the wall and began to snore at once. He was deep in sleep before the light of the rising moon had moved another half an inch across the packed earth floor of his *jacal*.

Hennepin came awake suddenly. Listening, he heard nothing. The village seemed unnaturally quiet. He knew it was very late by the length of the moonlight's fall into the hut of To-klani. He glanced over at Peckinpaugh and saw that the latter was wide awake, watching the doorway. Hennepin's eyes shifted. There was a shadow in the entrance way that had not been there five seconds before. The shadow moved—

stopped—moved again—froze. Seconds slipped by. A full minute passed. Hennepin blinked, and a human figure stood framed in the doorway where the shadow had been. The figure came into the *jacal*. It moved to To-klani's side, raised a short club it carried, then struck deftly. The blow fell behind To-klani's ear, and the old man sighed and went into deeper slumber yet. Next moment, the figure crossed the *jacal* and stood in the moonlight before Hennepin and Ben Peckinpaugh, the ancient Spanish padlock key from To-klani's neck chain dangling in its hand.

Could it be? Was it possible? Was this truly Cuddles, the thieving Lipan tracker, the traitorous red scoundrel who had stolen their horses and fled from them to save his own cowardly hide? Indeed, it was he. There could be no mistaking that monkey-like grin or, God bless him, that remarkable gift for shrinking a complex situation to size.

Said the little Texas Apache: "Come on, hurry up, me unlock chains, we all run like wind."

Freed of the collars, Hennepin and Peckinpaugh took up To-klani's rifle, gathered up a grass basket of supplies, locked the unconscious subchief into one of the dog collars, and were ready to go. Outside, they paused a minute to let their circulation restore itself to their legs, knowing a life's run lay ahead of them. There was still no sound from the village. The black beehives of the *jacales* lay dotted at rest upon the valley floor like sleeping buffalo. No smoke curled from the cold chimney holes.

"What time you reckon it is?" whispered Hennepin, shivering to the dawn chill of six thousand feet in September.

"Late," muttered Peckinpaugh, eyeing the grayness over the Capitáns. "Damned late."

Said Cuddles, narrowing the observation: "Talk too much. Let's go."

156

* * * * *

Once past the last field and *jacal,* they swung into a dog-trot. Peckinpaugh followed Cuddles; Hennepin brought up the rear. None of them spoke further. Without horses and with daylight but an hour away, there was no time for conversation—or any need for it. Cuddles was heading due south-west, into the gorge of the creek. That meant a climb, and a cruel climb. They began it in continued silence. Heart, hand, lung, and limb seemed strained past all endurance in the next fifty minutes, yet as the rose-red sun tipped the Capitáns, they stood panting two thousand feet above the floor of Soldado's hidden valley and knew they had won the first of their run for life.

"Wagh!" grunted Cuddles, gesturing downward.

Far below, the Mescaleros were just swarming out of their *jacales* and running for their ponies. The escape had clearly been discovered, and the remainder of the race was on.

"Come on," Cuddles waved, signifying as much. "By Yosen, him good thing me still got horse!"

"What?" shouted Peckinpaugh. "You saying you still got our horses?"

"You bet. What do you think me do all this time? Me got more than horse, too. Come on, you see."

"¡Madre!" said Peckinpaugh. "You're amazing!"

"And you heap old fool. Me tell you that back by Mesilla. Red Hair remember me say that back there."

"Sure," said Hennepin happily. "You said he couldn't smell an Indian no more without he had a bloodhound to help him. But let's get going for them horses. The Apaches ain't waiting for breakfast down yonder."

The Mescaleros were riding out of the *ranchería* now, but in the wrong direction, away from the creek gorge. Cuddles's homely face darkened. "Me no like. Bad, bad," he said.

"Bad?" challenged Peckinpaugh. "Why, it's good! They're heading the wrong way. It's you that's losing your smeller for red meat, not me, blast it!"

Cuddles looked at him. "Apache never go wrong way, Old Horse," he said. "We still got run like wind."

Minutes later, the tiny Lipan brave led them into a meadow no larger than a corral. They saw their horses standing saddled and waiting, but they saw something else waiting with the mounts—someone else, rather.

"*¡Madre mía!*" said Ben Peckinpaugh. "It's Pilar!"

It was. But there was no time for explanations. Pilar rode Cuddles's black Indian plug. Hennepin took his bay, Peckinpaugh his old roan. Cuddles led the way on foot and at a loping wolf's gait, a gait that the Lipan could hold longer than any horse. The track plunged downward into a dark gorge. Time and again it seemed to leap off into empty space. But always they negotiated the terrible curves and continued. It required but thirty minutes to reach the comparatively level and good going of the cañon's floor far below. Here, between creek fordings and boulder detours, Pilar was able to fill in briefly her part of the strange escape.

After her capture, she said, Soldado had taken her from Kahtanay. The chief had treated her as an Apache princess, and, except for the resentment caused by his taking her from Kahtanay—a direct violation of tribal law—her time among the Sierra Blanca Mescaleros had been interesting, even exciting. But with the capture of Hennepin and her father, all had deteriorated in white relationships in the *rancheria* of Soldado. Kahtanay had been able to convince a large part of the band that Hennepin and Peckinpaugh were spies, the advance guard for the Pony Soldiers. Soldado had been forced to spirit Pilar away and hide her in an ancient cliff dwelling in this same cañon they presently followed. Then, the past midnight, Cuddles had come to the cliff dwelling, by what route or what knowledge only the little Lipan knew. He had gotten Pilar down out of the pueblo of the ancients and brought her to the meadow where the horses were hidden. As for the rest of it, she had done nothing but hold onto the ponies until Cuddles got back.

"Well," said Ben Peckinpaugh, "it's plain we all owe Cuddles more than we can ever pay him. What he did is something past belief. For thirty-seven days he's lived and kept three horses fat within five, six miles of near two hundred Mescalero Apaches. I ain't never heard of a piece of scouting to match it in forty years. It's hard to buy."

"It surely is," said young Trooper Hennepin with unexpected acidity, looking accusingly at Pilar Peckinpaugh. "How come you didn't cut and run, Apache Princess, when you had the chance in that cliff dwelling? Why, it's only a few more miles on into Ruidoso, and all downhill."

"Oh, sure!" Pilar laughed, green eyes flashing. "And it's only a few feet from the dwellings to the floor of the cañon . . . like maybe thirty feet . . . and likewise all downhill."

"Huh?" said Hennepin, blinking like an owl caught in harsh sunlight.

"Soldado took the cliff ladder away when he left me alone, Mister Hennepin. That suit you for an excuse?"

Evidently it did, for young Trooper Hennepin just bobbed his red head and followed the rest of them off down the cañon, feeling his first defeat at the soft hands of a woman.

Shortly, they came to the last bend in the cañon before the site of the cliff dwellings. The heat of the day was mounting, and the horses needed water and a pause to loosen cinches and blow out a bit. While his three companions dismounted and walked off the saddle cramp, Cuddles led the mounts to the creek side. Hennepin, idly watching him, saw a fleeting shadow of movement above the Lipan tracker. His eyes leaped cross cañon to a headland of granite cropping out from the far wall where a tributary creek spilled down into the main stream.

Atop the headland sat four dozen Mescalero horsemen.

Hennepin cried out in warning and ran forward. As he did, Kahtanay's rifle cracked, and Cuddles spun twice around and went down in the creek shallows. Instantly a storm of Apache fire pelted into the freed horses. This eagerness to shoot the mounts of the escaped prisoners momentarily saved Hennepin. The young trooper pulled Cuddles from the water and, slinging him over his shoulder, raced for the boulder behind which Pilar and her father had taken cover. Indian lead now smashed at the creek gravel beneath his flying feet, but he reached the boulder without a scratch. Cuddles was not so lucky.

The Lipan tracker had a hole in his abdomen that would accept a thumb to the base knuckle without stopping the pumping of dark blood. There was a decision to make: take the faithful Texas Apache with them, or let him lie where he was? Across the cañon, now, the Mescaleros were sliding their ponies down the headland trail. Kahtanay, yelling them on, was baying like a buffalo wolf. The last, best chance seemed to be to make a run for the ancient cliff dwellings Pilar had described as being just ahead. Ben Peckinpaugh turned swiftly to Trooper Hennepin.

"Pick him up," he ordered. "We'll go down together."

Hennepin reached unquestioningly to raise the tiny Lipan, but Cuddles had reached a decision of his own.

"No, Red Hair," he pleaded. "Me feel cold in belly. Cold in leg. Me already dead, boy." He glanced up at Peckinpaugh. "Old Horse," he gasped, "you tell boy me claim Apache law."

160

The white-haired scout knelt beside him. "You sure, old friend?" he asked.

Cuddles nodded weakly. He held up a pathetically small, dark hand. "Yes. You take hand for good bye. Last time."

Peckinpaugh put his arms about the Indian and held him close for a moment. When he stood up, the tears were coursing down his gaunt cheeks. "He's got his rifle and can still see to shoot it," he told Hennepin. "It's the Apache law that we got to leave him behind to defend our lives, if he asks it."

"No, sir, Mister Peckinpaugh," said Trooper Hennepin, "we can't do it. It ain't human!"

"Neither are *they*," answered the old scout, pointing to the yelping Mescaleros. He gave Pilar a starting shove. "All right, girl, run for them cliff houses! We're right behind you."

But Pilar would not run. "I'm staying with Hennepin," she said.

"Oh, good Lord!" groaned the latter, "you can't do that. Go on, run! I'll go with you!"

They were all running then. Behind them, they heard the bark of Cuddles's Volcanic rifle. The sound was immediately drowned out by the heavier blasts of the Apaches' Springfields and Maynards. But it was evident from the angry cries of the Mescaleros that the dying Lipan tracker had brought the pack to bay. And by the time its savage members had rushed the big boulder behind which he lay, Cuddles was grinning his last grin straight up at the morning sun. He did not feel the slash of the knife wielded by Butcher that took his hair. Nor did he hear the animal snarl with which Butcher ripped the pitiful trophy loose and raised it over his head.

The last thing Cuddles remembered was Old Horse Peckinpaugh gripping his hand and calling him "old friend." In what better memory might a very small man die?

It was so quiet in the cañon that the white fugitives in the cliff ruins could distinctly hear the buzzing of the deer flies pestering the Apache ponies across the creek. And it was hot. It was so hot it made Butcher's spittle fry on the rock where he lanced it in disgust at the stalemate. Kahtanay, sharing his position, picked up a pebble to suck upon. *"Dah,"* he said, "it's no good," and went back to watching the silent ruins above. Little Pig lay in the shade of an alder clump, tossing rocks into the creek, leaning down for a cool drink whenever he wished it. He was not interested in watching the cliff. He whistled back at the cheery mountain blue jays, picked his teeth with the point of his knife, wasted not a worry on the foul hunting luck that had allowed the white people to reach the ancient pueblo and to draw up the cliff ladder behind them before the Mescaleros might catch them.

Soldado, sitting with To-klani in the rocks upstream from the ruins, said to the old man: "What shall I do?"

Replied the grizzled elder patiently: "Do nothing."

They waited.

On the cliff above them, the two white men and the rescued girl knew that their position, if less than happy, was far from hopeless. Peckinpaugh and Hennepin had been gone from Mesilla nearly six weeks. Major Ash would long since have had a column in the field looking for them. The soldiers would be sure to come to this cañon in time. As for food, they had plenty, both from To-klani's *jacal* and that which Soldado had left with Pilar. There was a good spring in the rear of the pueblo cavern. They were in a better situation for waiting than were the Mescaleros. One problem remained: prove this fact to the Apaches.

Said Hennepin, after talking the whole thing through: "Mister Peckinpaugh, what we going to do?"

Answered Ben Peckinpaugh in the same spirit as another old man had answered another young one only moments before: "Hold our water."

High noon came and was burned under by the relentless sun. The temperature at streambed was over 120 degrees. Mid-afternoon: the heat, thickened by the sun bake of the east wall, grew stifling. Apache lips began to wither, noses to dry and become glued shut, tongues to swell and shut off breathing.

"I must go to the creek and get water," panted Butcher to Kahtanay. "I feel the heat sickness coming on me."

Kahtanay looked at his friend. He saw the gray of shock spreading in his face. He felt his hand, and it was cold. There was only a dribbling pulse of blood at his wrist. "Go ahead, hurry," he said. "I will give you cover."

Butcher vomited before he could rise to leave. He wove with weakness toward the stream. On the cliff shelf, Peckinpaugh heard the disturbance. "Hand me them field glasses," he snapped at Hennepin.

Handing him the battered glasses that they had stolen from To-klani, the trooper's eyes narrowed. "That's Butcher," he said. "Don't miss him."

"If I do," gritted Peckinpaugh, "Cuddles will never forgive me. That's the Lipan's hair dangling at Butcher's belt."

The carbine loomed, and two hundred yards downstream Butcher leaped spasmodically, ran a few steps, only to fall sprawling.

"Heart shot," said Peckinpaugh, lowering the gun. "Jump, run, drop dead. He won't twitch a toe."

"Neither will you, if you don't get down off that wall, Mister Peckinpaugh," warned Hennepin.

"I reckon that shines, Red." The old scout grinned and moved to obey. But he moved too late. Kahtanay's rifle was

163

on him, and the bullet slammed Peckinpaugh twice around and down to his knees. Hennepin fired three times at Kahtanay, but was only splashing lead on rock and understood it.

When his shots reverberated off into the reaches of the cañon, the silence held for perhaps three long minutes. Then Soldado spoke. "How bad is the old man hurt?" he called up to Hennepin.

"Not too bad," replied the trooper carefully. "Why?"

"Because if he can live a few days, you will win. We learn only now that the Pony Soldiers come this way soon." He paused significantly. "Five days maybe. Can Old Horse wait that long?"

Hennepin knew that the old scout could not wait even one day. If he did not have the skilled nursing that only the Apache women could provide, he would die. Hennepin suspected that Soldado knew this very well. There was a certain way a man spun when he was deeply hit, and the Mescalero chief had seen Peckinpaugh grab his belly and go twisting down.

"Old Horse can wait," he said at length to Soldado, but he had taken too long to say it.

"*Wagh!* Good," answered the young chief. "So can we."

The silence returned then and did not alter. The day wore on, a cañon oven of flies and heat and pony stink. Darkness came at last, and, with it, Ben Peckinpaugh commenced to talk irrationally. They could not silence him, and the fever rose with each hour. Pilar and Hennepin went, about nine o'clock, to the front wall and inquired of Soldado as to his terms for a possible truce.

"We will take Old Horse and nurse him," said the chief. "You, Red Hair, may go free. This in exchange for the girl, Pilar. She is claimed by Kahtanay and by me. But if you want

164

to fight me for her, Red Hair, that is our law. If you win, you take the girl and all that is mine in this life, including my life. If I win, I take these same things from you. This is a thing the headmen have just voted on, Red Hair, a matter of the tribal honor. Kahtanay and I shall decide between ourselves at another time. What do you say?"

"I don't know," admitted Hennepin. "I must have time to think."

"Don't be a fool, boy," barked old To-klani, coming into the exchange testily. "We can hear Old Horse breathing all the way down here. He sounds as though he had been cut into by a dull wood saw. You had better let us take him tonight. We can throw you some rope and you can lower him to us."

"Well, if I do, how do I know you will do as you say?"

"You don't know," growled To-klani.

Ben Peckinpaugh was now unconscious. Hennepin turned to Pilar and asked uncertainly: "What shall I tell them?"

The slender daughter of the old scout moved past him to the wall. "To-klani," she called down. "Throw up the rope."

Twenty minutes later Peckinpaugh was in a pony litter moving up the cañon trail for the *ranchería* of Soldado on the far side of Sierra Blanca.

Hennepin waited for the dawn. His tacit agreement to meet Soldado in combat kept him from sleep. He did not feel good inside. He did not think he was afraid, really, yet his limbs felt weak. He looked over at Pilar. She seldom stirred, sleeping as a child, easily, gently. Hennepin reached across her to pull the blanket higher against the desert chill. What a crazy ending this was to his soldiering time. He wondered if he had been asleep the entire adventure, from the San Miguel raid to this moment in the ancient cliff ruin. Would he awaken to find himself back in his tent outside the headquarters adobe in Mesilla? Had he ever left the 3rd cavalry encampment? Was Cuddles still alive, Peckinpaugh unwounded, Pilar still safe at the family *hacienda* outside San Miguel? Did Soldado exist? Were Kahtanay or Butcher or To-klani or Little Pig real? Apaches? Was Hennepin's hair red, Pilar's eyes gray-green? Was anything as it seemed?

He awoke with a start. The sun was slanting into his eyes over the eastern rim of the cañon. Pilar's hand was on his shoulder. Her soft voice was urgent.

He stumbled to his feet and stood staring down over the stone wall of the ruin, into the cañon bed. The chill spread along his spine. The Mescaleros were waiting for him. The fighting ring was ready down there. On the far side of it stood Soldado, arms folded across chest, naked to the waist, looking calmly up at him. The young chief's face was neither angry nor encouraging. Fifty warriors flanked him, chanting a song of their people's honors and traditions of the *duelo a muerte*. Behind Soldado were his two friends, To-klani and Little Pig. And behind them was Kahtanay, fierce-eyed, aloof, waiting.

Hennepin put the ladder in place and slid over the lip of the wall, feeling for the rungs. He went down praying the Indians would not see the tremble in his legs, the quivering in his hands, as he walked toward them.

The Apaches watched him come. It seemed to them that the tall red-headed boy walked well enough. He stood straight, and, if he came slowly, he came without evidence of great fear. It appeared as though he might die well enough.

To-klani, who would be the referee, stepped forward. He held two wooden-handled common butcher knives. Seeing the naked blades, Hennepin shivered in the morning sun.

He had known it would be with knives. That was the Indian's weapon. The Indian grew up with the knife, as the settlement white boy grew up with his father's gun. It was as natural to the Indian as it was alien to the white man that combat should be made with edged steel. But Hennepin hated knives. He was not good in using them. He believed them vicious weapons and unfair. He had never employed one in self-defense and knew, as he walked into the Apache circle, that should he use one now he was already dead.

Another way must be found.

And, in the half minute of his walk across cañon floor into the Apache circle, Hennepin found it. When To-klani came over to him and offered him the second of the two butcher knives, the first having been given to Soldado, the young trooper took it and flung it into the creek, saying: "I will not take knife against a brother. Soldado and I have touched our hands. We have pledged our hearts as brothers. I shall fight Soldado only as a man . . . without weapons . . . with the hands, *mano a mano.*"

An ugly murmur at once ran the Mescalero ranks. This was not a good thing. Red Hair had tricked their chief. Yet honor was involved—the tribal pride—and there was no way out.

Soldado saw this as soon as his fellows. Pausing only to raise his hand and still the Apache anger, he threw his own knife into the stream and said: "It shames my *jacal* that my white brother had to remind me of our pledge. Blame my love for the girl, Red Hair. We will fight as you say."

"All right, all right!" complained To-klani irritably. "Let it be *mano a mano,* but begin it *now!*"

When the old Indian referee said that, and the surrounding warriors growled quick agreement, Hennepin knew the way that it must begin and end. He stepped into Soldado's gliding approach and smashed the Apache youth into the creek rocks with a right hand that went into the Mescalero's handsome face with the force of a rail-splitting maul. Soldado got up, shaking his head and spitting blood but making no sound. He came back at Hennepin with a rush this time. The trooper gracefully side-stepped and smashed him down into the water-polished stones once more. Again the Indian leader forced himself to his feet, again came at the waiting white youth. And it went like that from shocking first to brutal last. There was not a sound save the splintering blows of Hennepin's big fists, the grunting of the breath being driven out of Soldado's muscular body, the roll and rattle of the rocks as the Apache went down into them or pushed his way back up out of them. Five minutes may have passed, no more, before the Sierra Blanca chief was beaten senseless. And Red Hair Hennepin was standing over him with his breath coming easily and no mark at all upon his white-skinned body.

The Apaches sat in absolute silence. They had never seen a thing like this wrought upon a chief with the bare hands only. It was frightening—and more than that, there was something unclean about it, something indecent and bad. It as an obscene thing, and wrongful.

A low sound ran the Indian circle. It had almost a sorrowful undertone. It made Hennepin ashamed, somehow.

Eskim-azan, who had crushed the head of a little white girl with his rifle butt that same summer, got up and went for his pony without a word. Nakado-zinny, who had cut out the tongue of the little girl's mother because the mother cried too much over the child's life, followed Eskim-azan. Gato, who was called Cat because he would torture anything alive, and Gatho, his full brother, whose crimes of white and Mexican murder were notched into his Springfield stock from trigger guard to butt plate, arose and stalked off after their fellows.

Kahtanay went next, and that started the exodus in earnest. The tribal honor was shattered into a hundred shards of broken pride. *Wagh!* The Sierra Blanca Mescaleros had been humbled. Even Kahtanay would no longer look at the fight's prize, at the light-haired girl, Pilar. Forty-six Apaches followed him up the cañon and away from the bad place. Within a quarter hour of the fight's beginning, young Trooper Hennepin stood alone on the rocky banks of the nameless small steam in the Lost Cañon of the Ancient Ones.

Or, rather, he thought he stood alone.

"Well, boy, come on now," said a scratchy voice behind him. "Don't stand there all morning. There is much to do."

"*Anh,* yes!" added a second, more cheerful, voice. "Come help us wash off your brother in the creek water."

Hennepin wheeled to face old To-klani and good-humored Little Pig. True to their defeated chief beyond any possible insult to the Apache ethic, whatever Yosen, the Mescalero Almighty, might have in store for him, their action, taken in the face of the full band's censure, was a very brave thing. Hennepin now saluted them gratefully.

"*De nada* . . . it was nothing." To-klani shrugged. "When I love a man, I do not turn my back on him. Soldado has been a son to me, and I love him like a son."

"I, too, love Soldado," piped Little Pig. "But he's too big for a son. I think I'll call him a brother the way you do, Red Hair. All right?"

As Hennepin nodded, To-klani came over to him and put a wrinkled dark hand on his shoulder.

"Listen to me, white boy," he said. "I know why you threw away the knife. It was to save Soldado's life. You might have killed him, and to prevent that thing happening you threw away your weapon."

"Never!" denied Hennepin. "I was frightened gray!"

"Of course, you were. Yet you gambled with your life in spite of your fear. That is real bravery. I understand it, even if Kahtanay and the others do not. They are all too busy thinking of how to kill white men, how to waste lives, also. Or that it might be better to have peace than war."

"Sure! You say true!" agreed Little Pig, proud of his limited English. Then, slipping as easily back into Spanish: "Come, *amigos*, let us carry Soldado over to the water. *Hola*, Pilar!" He called across the creek to Peckinpaugh's pretty daughter, now scrambling down the cliff ladder. "We have some woman's work for you over here. Bring your soft hands to help our chief."

At the stream, Pilar took over the washing of the Mescalero youth's abrasions, doing the chore with all the natural skill of a born Sierra Blanca Apache girl. Hennepin, watching her with frank admiration, thrilled as well to the grace and beauty of the figure that the settlement girl made kneeling at creek side in the cañon sunshine. With her gray-green eyes and taffy-colored hair, set off by the dark creamy skin, she was, he thought, easily worth the risks that he and Ben Peckinpaugh had run to find her and to take her back safely to San Miguel. But it was this very thought, crossing the young trooper's easing mind, that now straightened his shoulders and brought the frown back to his freckled face. It had not been Pilar Peckinpaugh they had been sent to find and take back to San Miguel, but Soldado, and to the 3rd cavalry encampment at Mesilla!

As soon as the Mescalero chief's mind had cleared completely and Pilar finished with cleaning his injuries, Hennepin put the burden of his belated memory into hesitant Spanish.

"Hermano mio," he said, "I am sorry for what has happened here. I fought you like an animal, without the honor of

170

weapons. Yet death does make cowards of each man and every man."

Soldado looked at him curiously. There was no rancor, no racial hate, in his calm surveying of the red-headed youth. He seemed surprised more at the eloquence of the other's speech than at the nature of its content. It was not often that an Apache heard a Pony Soldier address anyone in a manner at once so *simpático* and *sentimiento*. He touched his brow toward the trooper.

"*Mil gracias,*" he said. "Do you know, Red Hair, that I could not have killed you, either? Kahtanay and the *Hesh-ke* insisted that I fight you, and that I kill you. But I, too, would have thrown away my knife, when the moment came. You are right. We are all women when death stares our way."

Hennepin awkwardly raised his hand. "We understand one another, *schichobe,* old friend," he said. "But now we must talk of the ending. We must remember why Old Horse and I came to your *ranchería.* Do you recall?"

"You speak of returning with you to Mesilla?"

"Yes. Major Ash thinks that, if you will speak for the Mescaleros, peace will come."

"You mean, war will not come, do you not?"

"Yes, I guess that's it. Will you come with us?"

"What good will it do? Do you think Kahtanay and the *Hesh-ke* will listen to what I promise the Pony Soldier chief?"

"Major Ash thinks they will. Old Horse told him you were the head of the band that was making the raids. Major Ash told us to find you and bring you in to talk peace."

Soldado nodded and sighed with great weariness for one so young. Hennepin could not understand it. To him, things appeared to have broken nicely. Peckinpaugh was getting the best of care at the Sierra Blanca *ranchería.* Pilar had been recovered unharemd, and 3rd cavalry troops were in the field nearby. It was only a two-day downhill walk out of the cañon to Ruidoso and the safety of the settlements. Soldado, if licked handily in a fist fight with a white man, was still chief of the Sierra Blanca band, still head of the Mesilla Valley Mescaleros, still the man Major Sanford Ash wanted to see and had to see in order to get an Indian peace agreed on.

"Why do you hesitate, *amigo?*" he asked the Apache youth.

Soldado sighed again and shook his dark head.

"I know my people, and I know your people," he said. "But I will go with you, Red Hair, because we are brothers."

"Yes," added Little Pig airily. "We are all brothers, except To-klani. He is too old. He will have to be a father."

"Surely," said To-klani, "no gourd makes so much noise as that one which is empty."

"Oh, yes, excuse me," added the fat brave, "I forgot about Pilar. She can't be a brother, either. She will have to be a sister, I guess. Unless Red Hair wants to take her to the blan. . . ."

"Fool!" cried To-klani. "Be still! Gather up the things and close your mouth. Pilar, you take my pony. Red Hair, you use Little Pig's scrubby runt. The fat one and I will walk." He paused, lowering his voice. His hand went to his chief's arm. "Come on, Soldado, we are not afraid, you and I," he said. "Let us show the Pony Soldiers how an Apache rides in."

The meeting of the Sierra Blanca chief, Soldado, with Major Sanford Ash of the 3rd cavalry was a travesty upon all Indian/white peace talks. The Apache leader and the Army officer reached an entire understanding, settled absolutely nothing, and parted with no idea in the New Mexican world how either would bring his respective people to abide by the meaningless handshakes, touchings of the pen, and pathetic expressions of "good heart" with which they bade farewell to

one another that golden September sunset outside the headquarters adobe in Mesilla.

Nor was that the only irony of it. For his part in bringing in
the hostile Mescalero chief, Trooper Hennepin was made a
first sergeant, earning with the rank the right to have a wife on
post at Fort Mimbres. The wife, of course, would be pretty
young Pilar Peckinpaugh, and for the dowry of good fortune,
which he might otherwise never have known, he could thank
his Apache brother.

As for Soldado, Trooper Hennepin could scarcely bring
himself to watch and listen to the Apache chief in his final appearance before a United States military command. The difference between this humbled, awkward, and ill-spoken
"peaceful" Soldado and the magnificent wild youth, with the
"look of mountain eagles" shining in his fierce face, whom he
had met upon the mountain high above his secret *ranchería*,
was a devastating thing to see. It made Hennepin want to
weep.

Major Sanford Ash did not see it. Captain Prescott, Lieutenant Carter, and Post Surgeon Bellamy did not see it. None
of the staff saw anything but the "miserable, ignorant savage"
who had killed four good men at Doña Ana and carried off a
teen-aged girl from San Miguel. The sole exception to this
blindness of the time and place was Second Lieutenant
Hampton Huckabee, who everyone knew to be a simple sort.
As Hennepin left the council at Soldado's side, he overheard
Huckabee say angrily to Captain Hugh Prescott: "Oh, miserable, ignorant savage, my foot. Hugh! The poor devil was half
sick with shame and helplessness. He has more dignity, yes,
and good sense, by the Lord, in his little finger than you and I
and the others have in our whole stunted bodies. If you want
to know what you see going past you with Sergeant
Hennepin, yonder, it's a *man!*"

173

Hennepin walked with Soldado past the picket line, out to the edges of the sage and piñon, where To-klani and Little Pig waited with the Apache horses. He stood in silence as the Mescalero chief took his pony and swung up upon it. The hearts of both Soldado and himself were composing things to say, but the tongue of neither was able to say them. Something bad had happened just now in that soldier meeting. It was a thing far better left unspoken. Both of the youths knew this. Neither of them wanted the other to see that he did.

"Good bye, Red Hair," Soldado smiled, leaning down to give Hennepin his hand. "We have each done our best. If our people will not see it, do not blame yourself."

Hennepin shook his hand, gripping hard with feeling. But he could not say what he wanted to, even yet, and so said nothing. Nodding that he understood, Soldado turned his pony to depart. Hennepin started after him impulsively.

"Soldado!"

The Indian youth checked the nervous mustang. "Yes, my brother?"

Trooper Hennepin came to his stirrup fender. He put his bony, red-haired hand on the other's bronze knee. Then, even after that, he still could not say what he had wanted to say—that he was sorry, a thousand times sorry, at the way that it had gone and for his own sad part in the matter—and so he only took his hand quickly away from the dark knee and stepped back and said very softly: "It is nothing, my friend . . . go with God."

Soldado and To-klani and Little Pig made him the Apache sign of respect, with the fingers touching the forehead, and sent their ponies into a lope. At the last far bending of the river road, Soldado turned and waved to Hennepin. The young trooper never knew if the Mescalero youth saw his return wave, or, indeed, if Soldado ever reached his high and lovely mountain home again. The next day Kahtanay and the *Hesh-ke* began their Indian War along the Río Grande. The names of To-klani and Little Pig and Soldado were heard no more in the land. Red dust they were, and to the red dust returned. So, at least, runs the legend of Trooper Hennepin.

Rough Riders of Arizona

Prescott had not come on any vast amount, Pete decided, since he had last won the bareback money there three years ago in the summer of 1896. The saloons still began just beyond the stage office at Gurley and Mount Vernon and ran on from there.

Pete had heard it stoutly maintained that there were other enterprises than Gila juice mills in Prescott, but he questioned the idea severely. More whisky to his certain knowledge was drunk annually in that town than in the rest of Arizona Territory. They used it to chase their water with. Of course, to be fair, there was more whisky than water available. It was truly that dry in Prescott. There was naught save gray granite, white rock dust, and red-bark bull pines growing there. The creek was said to be damp for a part of certain years, but mostly it ran to ragweed, rusty cans, chicken-dusting puddles, and old bedsprings. It was needful, the natives said, to take on a quantity of liquid so as not to dehydrate and die of thirst right there among their neighbors. So they took no chances on such a terrible end.

Pete clucked to his pony. The wiry runt had recognized the town and had slowed down and tried to turn off into the Black Cañon road, toward Phoenix and Tucson. At least, down that way there were the Salt and the San Pedro rivers. With a camp shovel and a little digging you could bore out a water hole even in August. But here in Prescott you took the native drink or none at all. And the little grulla mustang shared his rider's distaste for bottled or barreled restoratives.

Ahead, now, coming into the main road from the Black Cañon direction, was another horseman. He, too, was dust-clad from hard travel. He carried two blankets, rolled behind his saddle, and was young and lean and from a long way off looked just like Pete. Pete's mustang raised her head and flagged her ragged ears toward the newcomers. The other mount responded with a friendly whistle-whicker of the kind peculiar to *mesteños verdados,* be they Pecos, Panhandle, or Yavapai bred. The horses now having announced their desert kinship, it remained for the riders to do likewise.

Pete slowed his mount, watching the other youth warily. After all, even within sight of the lights of Prescott, it was still a lonely country, one wherein the travelers of merging trails did well to keep an eye on one another's attitudes. But the stranger from the south was as hungry for a friendly word as ever Pete Easter. He, too, pulled in his mustang and came up to the meeting, watchful and on the *qui vive,* while getting ready to grin at the drop of a halfway well-meant hello.

"Howdy," said Pete. "Going to Prescott? I'm Pete Easter."

The other youth's narrowed eyes opened wide. "*Big* Pete Easter?" he asked, patently floored.

Aha! thought Pete. *Here is a man who has ridden a few trails. He knows what counts.* "Yep," he admitted, not even blushingly. "That's me. How come you to realize it?"

"Well," said the other, smiling in a fetchingly diffident manner, "first place, you ain't small."

Pete knew what size he was: six four and something to spare, with bones and muscles and gristle to match. He nodded a little curtly. Was this boy trying to stretch him on the fence to dry? "Yeah," he said. "What else?"

"I seen you take the bareback money three years ago. Fourth of July," answered the slight, shy rider. "Man, you was grand."

Pete swelled to at least six five. "Thanks," he accepted graciously. "Who'd you say you was?"

"Hecker," answered the other youth quietly. "Billy Hecker of Sonoita."

Pete let out his breath like a stepped-on toad. *"Billy Hecker of Sonoita?"* he repeated, awe-stricken.

"Yes, sir," said his companion, "the same."

Pete turned red, then white, then settled on a sort of sick medium-gray-green. Billy Hecker of Sonoita was only the greatest saddle-broncho rider in the Southwest, barring only maybe Tom Darnell of Deming or A.R. Perry of Phoenix. And, compared to bareback, saddle-broncho riding was the fancy frosting over the plain cake. Bareback just wasn't in a league with saddle-broncho. It was like salt sow to roast sirloin, or blue John milk to Jersey cream.

"Cripes!" managed Big Pete, inspired. "Let's ride."

In Prescott, they put up their horses at the livery stable of the stage line. Billy was overwhelmed with the grandeur of everything so far. When he had come to ride in the rodeo that Fourth of July three years ago, he had not stayed in town after dark. He had never seen a settlement bigger than Sonoita with its lights turned on all at once, and he could not adjust readily to such unadulterated splendor as the hub of Yavapai County after midnight.

Moreover, in the previous visit, he had been called on to accept just the normal holiday rodeo crowd in from the surrounding range country. Now, with Teddy Roosevelt having called for volunteers to join up in his private cavalry and go to whip the vile Spaniards in Cuba, why, hell, everybody in Arizona Territory that was anybody, and hale, was in Prescott waiting for the enlistments to start out at nearby Fort Whipple. There must be, Pete and Billy estimated, just by glancing up Gurley toward the Square, close to five hundred men milling around the plaza, yonder. And, by God, here it was coming up 3:00 A.M. in the morning!

Well, no wonder, thought Pete Easter, that a simple country kid like Billy Hecker was somewhat spooked by it all. It was a good thing he had an experienced guide with him, or he might have been stampeded. As for Billy, he seemed to accept his debt.

"Say, Pete," murmured the Sonoita boy, as they now came out of the stage line office, "just look it the length of that brand on this here livery stable."

Condescendingly Pete glanced at the sign. It was, in truth, a beauty. THE VERDE VALLEY & MOGOLLON RIM, NORTH PHOENIX, BUMBLE BEE, OAK CREEK, COCONINO COUNTY & SOUTH FLAGSTAFF STAGE LINE & LIVERY COMPANY was not, for a fact, the sort of business title to be ignored. Well, shucks, this was Prescott. A man had to be ready for such sights. Big city, big signs, that was all. But then, this Sonoita kid, famous broncho rider or not, was a real greenhorn, a hick. He wasn't to be blamed.

"Come on," said Pete Easter, gesturing toward the bracelet of lights encircling the plaza, "let's us go and scout the enemy."

Billy Hecker held back some. He hadn't much money, he said. As a matter of fact, he didn't have two thin dimes to rub together. Moreover, he was not a drinking man. His tastes ran more to horse liniment for horses. To this, Pete agreed.

"Sure, Billy,"—he shrugged—"me likewise. Whisky and me got no mutuality whatsoever. But, man, you got to see

Prescott with the lights turned on. It's something. Come on along. I got money."

"By George!" The other nodded. "I'll just go with you, Pete. It surely is fine of you to take me."

Flattered, Pete led the way. But without bourbon the tour turned shaky. It was, after all, 3:00 A.M. in the morning. At the 5,600-foot altitude the air cut like an Apache scalp-axe. When, after a turn of the sights along Whisky Row and Tomcat Alley, with detours to see the old log governor's mansion and the new all-stone courthouse, the wind began to rise and to whip the two young cowboys about the ears and to snap and rattle their horsehide vests like tissue paper. Pete and Billy decided they had had enough fun for one night.

Accordingly, Pete, the cosmopolite, suggested they seek out a suitable hostelry and bed down in style. Billy demurred, reminding his new friend that he had only eight cents to last him until Teddy Roosevelt and the U.S. Army took over his keep tomorrow, or whenever. Pete patted him on the shoulder and said the pleasure would be his. After some soul searching, the Sonoita boy agreed on the basis of considering the needed amount a cash loan to be repaid out of his cavalry salary. This arrangement having been shaken on, the two paladins angled across the plaza, taking more or less dead aim on an inn they had previously been impressed by. Not even Pete could recall, right off, another lobby in his enviable urban experience with such a rainbow of red leather armchairs, living green palm trees, and polished-bright brass spittoons. And, indeed, the Yavapai House was an imposing edifice—so much so, in directly upcoming fact, that when the two cowboys drew near to it, the younger lost his nerve.

"Pete," said Billy Hacker, "I got to tell you something. I ain't never been in no hotel in my lifetime."

Pete shrugged reassuringly, comfortingly. "Shucks," he

drawled, "that's all right, Billy. I been in two of them."

Billy Hacker nodded, not convinced. "I dunno," he said. "Look it that cussed whirligig doorway."

Pete threw a superior glance at the revolving glass entryway, the only one of its kind between Kansas City and San Francisco. "Pah, that's nothing," he said. "All the best places got them sort of gates nowadays. Come on."

He started into the door, unafraid, and Billy, gritting his teeth, stepped into the following quadrant as it came spinning around. Once inside, however, he broke and ran. Pete, taken by surprise and from the rear, was helpless. He and his comrade went whizzing around, crazy as squirrels in a cage.

Pete tried yelling and fanning with his hat to slow Billy down, but Billy had the bit in his teeth and would not be headed.

Once Pete tried leaping out of the door to save himself, but nearly lost his nose and one ear in the attempt. After that, he gave up and just kept running for his life. He was saved by a kindly old gentleman resident who got up from his snooze in one of the lobby chairs, limped over to the spinning door, stuck his face into it, and brought it to a jarring halt.

Pete helped the dizzy Billy out of his section, thanked their benefactor, starting for the desk. The night clerk, unamused by cowhands playing in his glass door at a quarter of four in the morning, told them that if they turned about and departed in comparative peace he would not press charges. But Pete pacified him by getting a rolled-up brown-paper sack out of his shirt front and showing him its contents—three $5.00 bills, a toothbrush, straight razor, picture of his mother, and sixty-three cents in small money. The fellow not only quieted down but rented them the primest room in the house. He said it was the Left Wing of the Presidential Suite, and he only charged them $7.50 for it.

Upstairs, they were much taken by the radish-pink, turquoise, and purple tulips of the carpet in the hallway, and also by the verdigris brass Rochester lamps screwed right into the walls. True, there was a dismal fragrance of some order, rather like sheep-dip or ringworm carbolic, but Pete believed that it was from the paste used for the gold and fuchsia wallpaper and claimed that it was a special imported "old-country" kind containing secret Egyptian ingredients that slowed down the vermin of one class and another and was used in all top-grade houses such as the Yavapai.

Billy nodded and said—"If you say so, Pete."—then added admiringly: "Lord, Lordy, seven dollars and fifty cents just for a place to bunk one night! My goodness, think of it! And you stood to it like Old Steamboat holding still for the bucking-strap. Jings, Pete! You got more innards than a scrub bull."

Pete, still trying to recover from the trauma of letting loose of $7.50 all in one piece, shrugged weakly. "It don't take nerve once you know how," he said.

"Man!" Billy beamed, uncooled. "Seven dollars and four bits, just like that! Wow-eee!"

They let themselves into the room and turned up the bedside lamp. The odor inside was heroic.

"It'll clear up soon as we pry open the window," declared Pete.

Billy coughed and nodded. "That must be top-quality paste, all right. It's a wonder it don't raise a blister in them walls. My, but it is stout!"

Pete muttered something general in return and headed for the window. When he had pulled it wide, a blank look came over his face. "Billy," he said. "This here ain't no winder."

"What on earth you saying?" asked his companion. "You must be mistook. If that ain't a winder, what's outside them oilcloth draperies?"

"It's a solid brick wall," said Pete. "They done set the winder frame smack against the building next door."

"By gum, Pete, we got to have air!" Billy's voice held a note of returning panic, and Pete tried gentling him quickly.

"Hell," he said, "we'll just prop open the outside door with this here chair and draw oxygen from the hall. There, that ought to do it. Come on, let's hit the hay."

Warily they got out of their pants, shirts, boots. They left their socks and hats on. The bed was skimpy and of hilly terrain. Billy surveyed it, backing uncertainly and pawing the board floor.

"That mattress," he declared, "is outer of order than the molars on a waffle-jawed mule. She is leppy-looking as a crock of Grandmaw's clabber."

"Naw, no such thing!" insisted Pete, feeling the landscape of striped canvas. "She's just full of goose feathers and duck fuzz, like all them high-grade ticks. Come on, pile in, partner."

He boarded the bedstead gingerly, fearlessly pioneering the way. But Billy remained standing in his drawers alongside the foot of it. He looked a good bet to bolt again, so Pete collared him with a yell before he could.

"Cuss it," he exploded, "get in here! Ain't I told you she's safe? What I got to do? Sign you a deed?"

Billy stood on one foot, cramping the toes of the other around his bony ankle. "It ain't that," he murmured, blushing. "It's that I ain't never slept with nobody afore now."

Pete sat up, staring at him incredulously. "Well, for Christmas sake!" he blurted. "It ain't like we was married, you know. Hell, I ain't never slept with nobody afore, neither, and I'm twenty-two years old! Now you pile in here and lemme cinch up this slinky blanket. The draft's blowing up my drop seat fit to pull off the buttons and flap me raw."

Billy blushed again but crawled in. He lay as far over on his side as he could without falling out on the floor.

"Douse the glim," ordered Pete. "She's over on your side."

Billy reached obediently for the table lamp. When the room was dark, there was a finely strained silence of some three minutes. Then Pete yelled and leaped bolt upright. Billy, inquiring as to his problem, was next instant giving a holler of his own. Scrambling wildly out of bed, he fell over the chair propping open the hall door. This mêlée managed to bring down, also, the bedside table and lamp. There were some further thumps and bumps and solid language involved in righting the furniture, firing up the lamp, and throwing back the bedclothes. They were, of course, too late. The invaders had retreated. Both victims, however, had recognized the enemy.

"Well," announced Pete, in roundup tones, "I done slept in too many line shacks not to call you the brand on that herd, Billy. We've been outrode by that slicker downstairs. What will we do?"

Billy was overcome. "Seven dollars and fifty cents," he mourned, shivering to the Arctic breeze whipping in from the hallway. "All that money for a stall without no winder and a humpback mattress full of bedbugs. It's purely sinful, Pete. And it ain't right, neither."

They were interrupted by an irate pounding on the wall between theirs and the adjacent room.

"For the luvva Gawd!" pleaded a weary voice, "shet up and go to sleep in there. It's four o'clock in the morning!"

Billy Hecker looked forthrightly at his comrade. "Feller's correct, Pete," he said. "It won't be more'n an hour or so to first light. You want to put out seven dollars and four bits an hour to get bed bug bit?"

Pete Easter reached for his pants. "Hell, no," he said, "let's ramble."

They dressed in swift accord. Before leaving the room, Pete rapped on the intervening wall and called out loudly: "Good bye, mister. You have drove us from our warm bed, and us but two orphaned boys what have been beat and bullied something merciless by a unnatural father and what are seeking their fortunes alone and unknown in the big city. We will all the same say a word for you in our prayers, sir."

The adjoining roomer called back for them to wait, that he had not realized their circumstances and that perhaps he could help them. But Pete was adamant.

"No," he cried, "it is too late. You have broke our spirits. Good bye, and go to Hades."

Downstairs, the clerk was no more elated to see them than he had been in the beginning. He made his ante before they had gotten off the staircase.

"You two give me one ounce of trouble," he threatened, "and I'll have the law here in thirty seconds. Jail's only around the corner, and the sheriff can hear me holler from here. And I can holler."

Pete smiled meltingly. "Shucks," he said, "no sense in doing that, mister." He eased across the lobby, still ducking his head and letting on as though in genuine pain from an overdose of the deep shys. "We only come down to take our money back," he added softly.

The clerk's mouth flew open to yell for help, but Pete had him by the collar before he could utter a sound. He hauled him out over the desk top and in behind a cluster of the potted palms. There he hung him up against the wall and started talking to him.

The old gentleman in the lobby only cocked an insomniac

eye in their direction, waved his cane in clear approval of the operation, and went back to his cat napping.

The clerk was a stubborn man and no coward. But Pete offered to lock him up in the same airtight cubicle he had rented them, and he broke down into a jelly of fear and went to begging for clemency. This he was allowed to purchase for $7.50, the exact amount Pete had given him for the Left Wing of the Presidential Suite. Putting the currency back into his brown paper sack, Pete promised that they would always have a kind word for the Yavapai House in their travels and that, if the clerk so much as put his nose out the lobby door when they departed, they would blow his head clean off.

It was a good standard threat, one Pete had read in a paperback thriller, and it worked just fine.

Neither the clerk nor his bowlegged guests took pause to consider that the latter bore no firearms of any description. It was just a statement that sounded right to both parties under the circumstances. It was received, as it was given, in good faith.

Out in the plaza once more, Billy Hecker suggested they go back down to the stage line office and sleep out in the livery yard behind same. They each had a blanket roll behind their saddles, and it was a certain way to save $7.50. Besides, argued the Sonoita boy, they would want some local information first thing in the morning as to the best and quickest way out to Fort Whipple—this, so they could count on being first in the enlistment line and not get left behind by being late to offer up their lives on the altar of sacred duty to their country. The stage line agent, old Mr. Shuffman, ought to be just the one to give them this local lowdown. Also, Billy had spotted a repair wagon out in the livery yard with a nice big cozy toolbox on its bed, which would make a dandy place to bunk down, up off the ground, and so forth.

"Now, then, Pete," the slim youth concluded anxiously, "what you think of that idear?"

Big Pete looked at his small friend in frank envy. "By Gawd, Billy," he said, "you don't talk often, but when you do take off, you're a finisher for sure."

"Yes, sir, thank you," said Billy. "What you think of my idear?"

"Well, sir," answered Pete honestly, "it ain't the prize winner of all time. I know this here stage line. They wouldn't give a lift to a dying man in the desert, without he had a round-trip ticket bought and paid for in advance. But I ain't got any better plan to offer, I reckon."

Billy Hecker grinned apologetically. "I know it ain't much, Pete," he said. "But it's a fact that repair rig with the big toolbox will work fair good. I figure we can shell the tools outen it and bed down in their place toasty as tickbirds on an old bull's rump. What you say?"

Pete, never chary with his largesse, banged him between the shoulder blades. "I say you're a forty-carat genius, by gum!" he enthused. "Come on, let's make tracks for the livery yard."

At the stage dépôt they crept around into the rear corral, or "yard" of the line. Here they located the repair wagon in a sort of brush *ramada* tacked onto the livery barn. It was no great work to toss out the various shovels, picks, axles, spokes, spanners, and whatnot of the wagon mechanic's trade, and so to ready their couch for what was left of the night. Securing their blankets and a couple of armloads of sweet dry hay, they first made mattresses of the hay, then snugged themselves into their blankets atop it and at opposite ends of the toolbox.

But sleep, so long delayed, now grew stubborn. Neither

youth could woo the muse, and so both fell into low conversation designed to prove to the other that he, at least, could do without rest indefinitely.

The flow of this talk was valiantly afield at first. It ran to bucking horses they had known, good fellows and bad among their rodeo confrères, prices of feeders and stockers and prime slaughter steers for the coming summer, the nutrient virtues of stem-cured hay as against cut-and-baled, what zesty ladies the Mexican females were if a man didn't mind a knife in the ribs, the best method of castrating a calf, the art of skinning rattlesnakes for belts and hatbands, how to set and throw a ground loop, hell catch, and figure eight with a show rope, and other such workaday vital statistics of their trade. But it was all mesquite smoke.

Soon enough they fanned it away from between them and got down to rolling second cigarettes and tackling the real topic, the war in Cuba. They agreed they weren't precisely sure what was going on between the U.S. of A. and Spain that called for a shooting fight, or why the Cubans had to be rescued by Teddy, or from what. But they were solid in their righteous rage over the Navy's recent court-of-inquiry findings about the blowing up of the battleship *Maine* in the Havana harbor, and equally worked up over the imminent prospect of being a front-line part of the 1,500-man Arizona contingent that was scheduled to be selected tomorrow and sent right on East as a separate, distinct unit of Colonel Roosevelt's cavalry. And they certainly agreed that the New York papers were entirely right, and that it was high time America opened up and showed the rest of the world that she didn't stand second at the trough to any of the other hogs, and for damned positive not to those mackerel-snapping Spaniard devils.

In this spirit of vaulting martial fervor, the two young men from Verde Valley and the Sonoita Plateau talked the stars dim, smoked up both sacks of Pete Easter's Bull Durham, and dropped off to sleep finally, just as the fighting chickens were beginning to crow over in Mexican Town, past the railroad yards.

When they awakened, it was to find the sun shining noon high in their eyes. Alarmed, they scrambled out of the repair wagon's toolbox, only to be met by an irate stage line agent who was not amused by the tools tossed in the manure of the livery corral or the cut hay borrowed for bedding from his rental barn. However, Pete was equal to the menace—or essayed to be.

"Why, good morning, Mister Shuffman, sir." He smiled. "It is charming to see you again. How has your arthritics been this spring?"

"You young fool,"—Abel Shuffman scowled—"how many times I got to tell you I don't want you nor your saddle bum friends bunking in my livery barn? Now you light outen here, Pete, and stay lit. I've a mind to send a bill to your daddy. What the hell you doing in town, boy?"

Pete told him. He added that he feared the hour was late, and that he and his friend from Sonoita would appreciate any guidance given them in the matter of getting out to Whipple Barracks.

"Do you mean," said old man Shuffman, "so's you can enlist in Teddy's Terriers?"

"It's Terrors, not terriers," corrected Pete patiently. "And yes, sir, that's what we aim to do."

"Well, boy, you'd better aim to do something else. During the night, President McKinley sent a telegraph message to Whipple, saying the number of Arizona volunteers had been cut from fifteen hundred to two hundred. I reckon you can count up what that did for the chances of your late-sleeping kind." The old man bobbed his head feistily at the stunned youngsters. "They had them two hundred men inside the first twenty minutes. And they opened the gates at sunrise."

Billy Hecker looked at his tall, tousle-headed bunkmate and said sadly: "You will have to excuse me, Pete, but there's something I got to say."

The big cowboy nodded miserably. "Go ahead and say it," he mumbled.

"Dad blast it!" said Billy Hecker.

They got their ponies and rode slowly out of the livery yard into Gurley Street.

At the edge of town they ticked their restless mounts with their spur tips, letting them into the rocking mustang canter that eats the trail miles. Minutes later, they pulled in at the forking of the Verde Valley and Black Cañon roads.

For an awkward ten seconds neither rider found words. Then Billy Hecker nodded stiffly.

"Pete, you ever get down Sonoita or Patagonia way, you look me up. Ask anybody in Patagonia where the Hecker place is."

Pete Easter returned the nod soberly. "Same to you, Billy," he said. "Providing you ever get over to Camp Verde or Cottonwood, our place is the Rafter J."

They exchanged a final set of nods and uneasy, shy smirks. Then they touched hat brims and rode on, one south, one east, neither of them looking back. The dust from their ponies swirled and blew a little in the midday heat, then that, too, disappeared.

River of Decision

While he was recovering in the post hospital at Fort Bliss from the nearly fatal leg wound he had received in the Confederate defeat at Glorieta Pass, young Jim Beau Travis had time to think about his affairs of the heart—to decide which girl it was that he truly loved and must return to when discharged.

He realized at last that he could not go back to Nah-lin, the slim Apache girl he had met while a captive of her fierce tribesmen in the New Mexico mountains. Wherever Nah-lin might have gone since Jim Beau's escape, whether or not she had married Solitario, the brooding young chief of the Dos Cañadas Apaches, Jim Beau must forget her, put her forever out of heart and mind.

He must remember only that he was a Travis—James Beaumont Travis, III, son and grandson of U.S. Army generals. He was, as well, despite his scant nineteen years, a commissioned officer in the Arizona Brigade of General Henry Hopkins Sibley, the Confederate pride of Texas. No youth of Southern honor could play off these stern facts of family and duty against his yearning memories of the Apache girl. Jim Beau understood this. He knew that no actual choice remained to him between dark-skinned Nah-lin and fair-haired Felicia Leeton.

The clear course of a Texas gentleman lay to cross the

parade ground to the homes of Officers' Row, where Felicia was residing with Major and Mrs. Phil Farraday. Jim Beau would take that course presently.

Meanwhile, he had checked out of his hospital ward and found an old Negro orderly who remembered Jim Beau's father, and his grandfather, and who was pleased to help the boy lieutenant carry his belongings to the Bachelor Officers' Quarters. And it was there the endless hours of the afternoon wore away. Night came on and deepened at last. Jim Beau gathered his courage, then, and set out across the parade ground.

It was a warm night, sweetly humid, with a hint of summer rain in its freshening west wind. Broken clouds drifted overhead, separated by patches of blazing stars. A fourth-quarter moon was climbing free of the rim of hills beyond the river. Its glow lit up the arid land, softening all its harshnesses, giving life and color to the naked rock and blighted mesquite. It touched, too, all who moved beneath it. It painted hale and halt, alike, with the same rich brush of moon fire. Jim Beau was grateful for that. He knew from the all-empty feeling within him that his face was white as a bed sheet, that he was yet a long way from well. Ordinarily a man would not permit his promised one to see him in such a condition. He looked like death warmed over and set aside to chill again. But toned up by the orange wash of that moon, he would not appear all that bad. Taking on the night's bright blue, he might even manage to look somewhat like the proud young soldier that Felicia Leeton had vowed to wait for.

Oh, nonsense. What was the use? He was only deluding himself. It wasn't that simple.

The pale youth slowed his step. Turning aside, he sat down on the small garden bench beneath the lone mulberry tree planted in the dirt yard at the head of Officers' Row.

Wearily he shook his head. He still knew precisely how he wished to make his appeal. It would be by telling Felicia the entire truth about himself, that his "vast ranch on Pecos Creek" was just so many barren miles of brush and thin grass, and that the "legendary Travis millions" had long ago been filtered away into the parched sands of his father's ruinous West Texas land speculations. Then he would tell her of his attempt to resign his commission and Sibley's refusal to accept it, then about his own determination to quit the brigade and go home even if it meant a court-martial. And lastly he would tell her of his lonely soldier's dreams that she would go with him to Pecos Creek to share whatever the luck of the trail might bring of great or small treasure, not caring which because they would have each other and be the wealthiest people in West Texas, come duster or downpour, good grass or bad.

Of course, he would say nothing of savage Nah-lin and of the strangely stirring time Jim Beau had spent as a captive of the proud Apache people—after Solitario had cut him off as he scouted too far ahead of the advancing Confederate column. But except for that interlude of primitive excitement, the rest of it was arranged in the manner he thought best to say it. However, the main difficulty remained. He must still find out how Felicia felt about it all. The only way to do that, unhappily, was to ask her. Jim Beau got unsteadily to his feet. He braced himself. Limping to the door of Major Farraday's quarters, he knocked hesitantly.

It proved to be his fortune that the Farradays were at a staff ball being given that night for General Sibley and his aides. Felicia was at home alone. When Jim Beau heard the remembered rustle of her petticoats and the light tapping of her silk slippers, he grew weak again. But then she had opened the door and was standing framed within the

195

golden square of its lamplight.

Jim Beau could only catch his breath and stare. "Hello, Felissy," he finally said. "It's me, Jim Beau."

He had prepared a thousand remarkable greetings for the moment, of which this was not one. It simply came out of him with native honesty. And it left him standing there suffocating with the anticipation of her glad cry of recognition, the heady perfumed embrace of long-separated lovers' welcome. He waited in endless, awkward vain.

Felicia Leeton only smiled archly. "Why, James Travis," she said. "Wherever in this wide world did you come from? We all heard you were dead or missing or something like that."

Jim Beau looked hard at her, peering to make out the set of her face in the lamplight. But she would not look back at him. He straightened. "Yes," he said, "something like that."

She waited, and he went on.

"I've been in the hospital, Felicia. I didn't tell them who I was until this afternoon. I wanted to spare you any bother or concern. How have you been?"

If she noticed he had dropped the pet name Felissy, she gave no sign. "Why, wonderful, just wonderful, thank you, James. Isn't it grand that you are back safely, you and all the other dear boys who fought so bravely up in New Mexico? It must have been frightful, just frightful."

Jim Beau thought of a Union artilleryman's face disfigured in the shotgun charge at Val Verde. He thought of the cruel saber cut a Confederate comrade had taken. He thought of another young Southern trooper shooting a cowardly officer of his own battalion six times in the back as the latter ran. He thought of the numberless fine young Texas boys and just as fine Northern boys left silent on the field, and of the others abandoned in their blankets at the camps of both sides, their features discolored by smallpox or contorted by tetanus.

He nodded and said very quietly to Felicia Leeton: "Yes, ma'am, it was frightful."

She moved nervously, trying to smile. "I do wish I might ask you in, James," she said. "But Colonel Mayberry is coming to take me to the ball. You remember the colonel, don't you? He's such a pet."

Jim Beau remembered Colonel Randolph Mayberry very well. He had never been near the battlefront. Also, next to James Magoflin of El Paso, he was the wealthiest man in West Texas and old enough to be Felicia Leeton's grandfather— almost. Jim Beau tried to keep calm.

"I remember him. What about him?"

"We are engaged, James. I'm going to marry him."

Jim Beau stood there. He wanted to go off and be sick. But he stood there. "What about you and me, Felicia? All those promises? All those dreams?"

"Oh, really, James!" Her voice turned petulantly patronizing. "You took the whole affair in San Antone too seriously. It was soldiers and uniforms, dances, buffets, wine, magnolias. Moonlight talk, James. It was wartime. We weren't serious. No one was. Nothing's broken between us that can't be put together again with a few more moonbeams!"

She laughed, easing the door against him, her eyes beguiling him with guarantees of tomorrow.

"You simply must run along, now, like a good boy, James. I'll see you in the morning. We'll arrange a little something for the evening. The colonel needn't know. He's such a dear, so trusting. Good bye for now, James."

She was closing the door yet farther. Jim Beau stepped quickly forward.

"Felicia!"

She hesitated, frowning. "Yes, James?"

He stared at her one last lifelong moment, getting the picture of her in his memory for final keeping. It was not a good picture. She knew it. She dropped her eyes, waiting for his bitterness to break.

"Good bye, Felissy," was all he said, and very softly.

At the Bachelor Officers' Quarters, deserted for the ball, it did not take him long to get out of his uniform and into his old scouting clothes. The feel of the fringed doeskin shirt, the worn leggings, and blunt Apache boots was medicine to his tired limbs. It turned his memory to the time he had spent as a prisoner among Solitario's fierce people. Life with the normal Apache had been a savage but remarkable experience. Jim Beau recalled it with particular nostalgia, it and the Indian people he had come to know: crusty old Nuñez, the senior headman, who said he hated everything and truly hated nothing; fat, foolish Chufeto, Nuñez's younger fellow on the tribal council who loved the world and proclaimed the affair at each opportunity; Chacal Delgado, Nah-lin's father, a Mexican Sonora Apache and a working bandit of the first wickedness. Then, too, there were Solitario himself, that aloof and lonely son of the old chief who now ruled the Dos Cañadas band so well and wisely in his dead father's image; and Grito, the vicious fighter and hater of the white man, head of the war party among the southern Apaches; and lastly and, of course, always, Nah-lin, the slim brown flame of the *monte,* the Apache girl with the face and form to fire the blood of any man—but, ah, what was the use of such wildly urgent memories? They belonged to the magic time of the past that he had spent with these sturdy red men of the desert. Such memories must be made to fade. They must be forgotten, given an Indian grave.

Jim Beau forced his thoughts to accept the Apache past. Resolutely he folded the tattered gray officer's blouse.

Placing it on the foot of his cot, he laid across it the sword John Baylor had given him with his lieutenancy at Mesilla. For a long moment he studied the blouse, memorizing its two rows of seven gold buttons, standing collar, and wide cuffs made stiff with the braid of his rank. Someday he might want to recall these things—the weapon and the uniform of his highest service to his heritage; a man could not know for certain of such things, and so Jim Beau lingered.

Then, with quick, self-conscious impulse, glancing first to see that no one had entered behind him, he saluted the forlorn gray blouse and tarnished blade. The rest went swiftly and with more ease.

Belting on the Colt revolver, he closed the drawstring of his old rucksack, picked up the Confederate carbine, and started down the moonlit aisle of the barracks. At the exit he hesitated, held by a last stray nudging of the life that had been. The frown lines on his sober young face intensified, then smoothed and seemed all at once resolved, rested, determined.

Under the kerosene lamp illuminating the exit way stood a tough plank table bearing the B.O.Q.'s library. The dusty books ran the frontier Army post gamut, from yellow paper editions of Cooper's THE RED ROVER and THE PATHFINDER to morocco-bound sets of Greek philosophy and Edward Gibbons's DECLINE AND FALL OF THE ROMAN EMPIRE. Somehow the collection did not seem complete to Jim Beau. An expression of regret twisted his mouth. From the rucksack he withdrew a slender volume that he had carried from Pecos Creek to Santa Fé and back. Not even looking at the small book, he placed it on the table and went out into the night. The book laid cover up, the sweat-stained gilt of its title gleaming faintly. It was THE PROFESSIONAL OFFICER IN COMMAND: HIS

OBLIGATIONS AND SACRED DUTIES AS A LEADER OF MAN. The author was his father, General James Beaumont Travis, II.

Outside, the moon was risen clear of the prairie hills. It was no longer dusky orange but white and weary-looking like Jim Beau. The latter glanced up at it uncertainly, noting the rain clouds gathering behind it and beyond the river. He could not know where that moon might lead him. Nor did he greatly care. He only knew he was going to follow it, away from Fort Bliss and away from his shameful career as a professional officer and leader of men. That was absolutely certain. In all the tragic months from San Antonio to Glorieta Pass he had seen the price of leadership paid over and over again, and always it was paid in the same bankrupt moral tender of human misery and suffering. Whether it was a tiny company of Confederate infantry scouts, caught in a Union rifle trap in the narrow streets of Mesilla, or a full regiment of gray cavalry shredded by blue cannon fire on the open plains of Val Verde, the terms of the final settlement were no different. To the leader of men, be he squad corporal, regimental colonel, or corps brigadier, the price of victory was the same as the cost of defeat—the lives of the men who followed their leaders. Jim Beau was no longer willing to pay that price.

Although his desertion would put the family name in disgrace, he must hold to his decision to do so. There remained only the choice of ways. As he stood trying to see this choice clearly, and to make it rationally, a gaunt shadow detached itself from the side of the barracks and glided soundlessly toward him. The next moment a deep, fondly remembered voice was murmuring Apache gutturals in his ear.

"If I were a son of my people," said the voice, "you would be a dead white man."

Jim Beau wheeled about. "Solitario, Solitario!" was all he could cry out, feeling so overcome, withal, that his throat closed tightly for the moment.

He took the young chief's hand in his and waited until the thickness in his throat dissipated. The Apache youth understood the delay. He was not the least embarrassed by it. After a little while he merely lifted his hand to Jim Beau's shoulder.

"Come along, my friend," he said. "We have been waiting a long time for you to get out of the sick house."

"We?" asked Jim Beau, puzzled.

"Yes, Solitario and some other friends of yours."

"But I don't understand. What other friends?"

"Those few of the Dos Cañadas band still loyal to me. We have decided to go away. We waited for you, hoping you would get well and come with us."

"Whatever are you talking about?" pleaded Jim Beau. "It doesn't make sense."

"I believe that it does. Much has happened while you have been sick. There is going to be a big war between the Apaches and the white men. General Sibley and General Canby both have issued notice that their two armies will henceforth shoot all Apaches on sight. This great danger has scattered my people. Grito has gone, with most of my band, to join up with Mangas Coloradas and the Mimbreños. For us few remaining ones it has become a question of to run away or get killed. So we are going far away to some secret place. We ask you to go with us, because we remember you. When your soldiers could have shot us, you ordered them not to fire, and we escaped."

"That was nothing," insisted Jim Beau. "It was for you not killing me as your prisoner long ago."

"The Apaches always pay their debts. Will you come with us or stay, white friend?"

"I still can't believe it," protested Jim Beau.

"You had better believe it. Our time here is brief as the hawk's shadow on the rock. My people are waiting for us down where the old road goes over the river."

"The Chihuahua Crossing?" said Jim Beau. "The ancient Indian road that leads all the way down into the Mexican Sierras?"

"That is the one, *schichobe*. I will not fight the white man. I am not afraid, but no war is ever won. I like you. That is why I call you *schichobe*, old friend in my tongue. But we can wait no longer for you. How do you decide now? Will you go and live with us?"

The thought was a desperate one, never really considered by Jim Beau Travis. But, of a sudden, its wild seed was growing within him. He threw back his head with a cry that was half shout, half laugh, and all joy. He stood as straight as the crippled leg would let him, feeling taller than the cloud bank of the coming rain.

"Old friend, *schichobe*," he said, "I will surely do it! I am so happy to see you that I would follow you off a blind chalk bluff. Lead on, but don't forget you've dabbed your rope on a pretty lame pony."

"Give me your packsack and your rifle," ordered the Apache. "Lean against me. Advise me if I go too fast."

Jim Beau obeyed him. They went across the parade ground to the river path. Presently they neared the old ford below Fort Bliss. Here it was that Jim Beau Travis came at last, and haltingly, to the hour of his own final crossing of that other river far wider than the silvered Río Grande. In the underbrush near the ford two saddled horses stood waiting. One of them was Solitario's nervous little paint stallion. The other was the trim steeldust mare, Paloma, that Jim Beau had ridden into the Dos Cañadas country to fall captive to the Apaches.

The young chief now led both animals into the moonlight. *"Schichobe,"* he said, "here is your horse."

"Thank you," said Jim Beau, but he could not move to take the reins of the graceful animal. Instead, he stood looking past his Apache friend, across the river.

Beyond the channel on the south bank, a small band of Indian horsemen sat, watching them. They made no sound, showed no movement. Jim Beau limped forward a few steps to get a better view of them. It was then he saw that they were not all horsemen. One of them, the slender, small, long-haired one, he would have known a mile away without moonlight. He drew in his breath.

Behind him, Solitario spoke softly. "Yes, it is Nah-lin, your woman, old friend. She has waited for you all of this time."

"My woman?" said Jim Beau with equal softness. "I would have thought she could be your woman long before this. Why has she not been?"

"She would not have it that way, and I would not touch the woman of a friend."

"Is that all?"

"No. It was she who first suggested that we wait for you. I said yes to her idea. So it is that we have waited and prayed that you would recover in time to go with us. Now we must hurry. It is very dangerous for us to stay, and not fair for you to require it of us by your hesitation." He swept the far bank with an eloquent gesture of his dark arm. "See, my white friend, over there are faithful fat Chufeto and fierce Delgado and wise gray Nuñez waiting for us. With them are those other few true-hearted ones of my old father's people who would not listen to the war talk of Grito. They will all be happy if you say yes, that you will come with us, but they cannot wait, any of them, much longer here for you."

"Let me think yet a moment," begged Jim Beau. "It is not as easy as I had thought to leave my other life behind me."

"It is not easy for us, either, white friend, to leave our old lives behind us. But come, I still hold your horse for you here. Do you want the horse? Will you take her?"

Jim Beau did not move to take the gray mare. He stared hard again at the silent blanketed figures across the river. Brought squarely up against their stillness, he was afraid.

He was not talking to another white man but rather to a pagan Apache Indian. And on the far shore other savages of the same untamed feral blood were waiting for him. With them waited the slender oval-faced Sonora girl, Nah-lin Delgado, as sun-black of skin, uncaged of mind, and wild in heart and thought as her dark-blooded companions.

Jim Beau brought his glance back to Solitario. His fears deepened. If he took the bridle reins of the mare, Paloma, from the Dos Cañadas chieftain and turned with the latter toward Chihuahua and the secret redoubt of the Mexican Apaches, he would have made an irrevocable decision—a decision that would require more real courage than his father or grandfather had ever shown in battle, a decision that would demand the moral will to abandon a lawful white society for an outlawed one, knowing the act made of him a frontier pariah for the remainder of his life. Nor was this even the entire depth of the matter. There was the underlying question of his military and patriotic loyalties. To see the truth about a cause, as he had seen the hopelessness of the Confederacy's struggle, and to renounce that cause before the facts of its failures were apparent to all took more resolve by far than to cling obstinately, blindly to it. Yet the final onus of such a renunciation was monstrous. There were many names for it, and the least of these was traitor.

If he accepted the gray mare from Solitario, he would be reduced to the jackal's status of an Army deserter. He would be a disgrace not only to his family but to every Southern family. If he received the mare willingly, the course must lead him into a life of brute nakedness, as the equal but scarcely the peer of the murderous broncho Apaches of the *monte,* the blood brother of cheerful killers, the accomplice of horse and cattle thieves, the mate, above all, of a woman whose pedigree was pure Apache, with no drop of civilized blood flowing in her veins. It was a decision to go over a river of no return. Jim Beau made that decision, now, and turned with it to Solitario.

Watching his white companion anxiously, the young Indian nodded quietly. "Well, *schichobe,*" he asked, "which way will it be? What must I do with this gray pony of yours?"

Jim Beau held out his hand. "Give the mare to me," he said.

Solitario, still unsure of the white youth's decision, surrendered the gray. Jim Beau smiled at him, then, with a sudden glad brightness. He stepped up on the mare, heart lifting as lightly as an eagle feather whirling upward in a sweet draft of desert air. He stood exultantly in the stirrups, filling his lungs with the night.

"Come, mount up, Apache friend!" he cried. "Let us ride over this wide river together!"

"With all of my heart!" answered Solitario, leaping to the back of his mustang. "Let it be always as you say, *schichobe,* riding like true brothers, side by side."

They put their mounts into the shallows of the old Chihuahua Crossing. Both horses were fresh, wanting to go. They made water-bright showers of silver droplets rise in the moonlight as they drove their hoofs into the clear green current of the Río Grande.

Across the stream, fat Chufeto bobbed his round head. "See how lovely the water looks falling every which way in the light of the moon," he said delightedly to his dour friend Nuñez. "Isn't that a nice and graceful thing to look at, Nuñez?"

"To the empty head," rasped the grizzled elder, "all such things seem agreeable. But, yes, I will grant you that perhaps you are right this one time . . . it is a nice and graceful thing to observe the water splashing in the moonlight. What do you think, Delgado?"

But the old Sonora bandit was not looking at the water or the moonlight. He was watching his slender daughter Nahlin. To him, her face appeared to shine far more brightly than the glancing moonbeam or the falling drop of water. But then perhaps Delgado was not grown too old to recall another night and another slim young Nah-lin in another time than this one, and he sighed happily even while putting himself on dignified guard against the suspicious glances of Nuñez and Chufeto.

It was not fitting that one with his reputation be caught in a trap of sentiment, but still he must not lie, either. "I think it is a beautiful night," he replied to Nuñez's question. "But we have already talked too much of it, and it remains a very long way that I must guide you down into the *monte*. Come on, spur up, old friends. Let us start on ahead of these young people and enjoy by ourselves this rain that is beginning now. We don't want to stay here and watch that foolish daughter of mine and that white boy, do we? *Pah!*"

Delgado raised his craggy head and sniffed the softly pattering drops. He held his wrinkled face to their melting touch. "Ah," he said. "Feel it kiss you. Does it not smell wonderful, the good smell of the rain?"

His companions nodded, and the three Apaches turned their ponies away from the Chihuahua Crossing. They did not look back, neither did Jim Beau Travis, nor did any of them come that way again.

Ghost Wolf of Thunder Mountain

I had the story from the lips of the man it concerned most. Therefore, I am confident in relating it.

This was in the Sangres country, when New Mexico was many legends younger than it is now. If I said the exact place was the ranch of Don Gaspar de Portogo on the Agua Piedra, certain *ancianos* would understand precisely what family and what *rancho* were intended. Yet, of course, the actual names would still be protected from today's pack of rasacls and trespassers, that collective amoeba of man's curiosity that will seep in any place where the Pale One has been before them. So, call the *rancho* Agua Piedra and its master Don Gaspar. And call the great mountain that towers beyond the river and the grassy slopes and the juniper flats El Trueno, because that is not its true name, either, but very close to it. Ah, Old Ones, do I see you nod and smile? Certainly. You know the peak I mean.

The season was early winter. The Christmas festivities had barely commenced upon my arrival, but at week's end had reached the carnival stage that we transplanted children of Coronado and Cabeza de Vaca regard as just the proper excitement for the Feast of the Christ Child.

Do not believe that the guest list was of far travelers and affluent, such as myself. Nothing like that. Don Gaspar was the *patrón* of an area larger than some states of the first American colonies. The good flock gathered at his elegant *hacienda* was composed principally of those he called "his children," and who in turn with vast respect addressed him as *el patrón*. These would be the *vaqueros* who guarded his castle, the *pastores* and *zagalos* who tended his sheep, the storekeepers, blacksmiths, cooks, and people of all degree who, with their broods of brown-eyed, beautiful little ones, and, of course, their buxom, white-toothed women were the "family" of Don Gaspar and of the Agua Piedra. But this is not their story—except in a related way, like the blood of brothers is related, while different, often to strange and violent ends.

On the night of which I tell, the merrymaking had achieved that riotous pitch that the Americans mistakenly called a *fandango,* a wild dance without morals and leading but to mayhem and marital as well as martial strife. Well, it was true some were dancing. And many, many were shouting on the dancers and the guitar and marimba players who lured them to their gay gyrations. If one added to this *baile* the shrieks and laughter of the children jousting to break the hanging clay baskets of bright gifts that decortead the rafters of the *sala grande,* Don Gaspar's great room in the *hacienda,* and also put into the sum of the uproar the clapping yelps of encouragement from the older ones who had passed the time of dancing in their lives, then a fact must be granted—something very like a *fandango* was going forward. But, then, these children of my own blood were not mingled with any but their own kind that evening. Only smiles flashed, and no knives.

Entering the *sala,* I searched at once for some less tumultuous haven. Presently I spied it: the far side of the room where the giant fireplace gave light and warmth to the eyes and bones of the oldsters clustered there, backs hunched to the gaiety behind them, reliving their own *bailes,* far greater than this one, complaining that in other days the children behaved themselves far more mannerly, and the young women, *por Dios,* would not dream of showing anything like as much ankle, calf, and—God bear it witness!—even *knee.*

Knowing this coterie from yesterday as the most compatible for a man of my persuasions and, yes, admit it, of better Christmases gone by, I made my way around the crowded wall. I had reached the hearth and found my seat beside a grandly handsome octogenarian *vaquero*—or had he been, indeed, *caballero?*—and was loading my pipe when it happened.

I had never heard such a sound before, or since. It was a long, quavering cadence of sorrow, indescribably mournful, and yet its burden came not into that room as sadness but as naked fear. Down it came through the silvered, hoar-frost air of the December night, falling from the bleak granite ramparts of El Trueno, Thunder Mountain, to spread like some chill from the other world among the gay dancers in Don Gaspar's *hacienda.* The pause was but that of an insatnt. There was a nervous shuffling of feet and coughing of throats and, here and there, a false, tittering laughter. Some young men, in bravado, spoke aloud. One child began sobbing. The older people were univresally silent. It was a very disturbing moment. It passed only because Don Gaspar alertly ordered the musicians to resume at once. This they did, with an irresistible rendition of *"¡Jalisco!"*

But the spell was not broken so swiftly that I had not time to note the peculiar action of the most grizzled of the graybeards by the fire. The old fellow had started up eagerly, as the great wolf's sobbing cry had echoed down the mountain, and he had remained in a tense attitude of listening long after the final eerie note had quivered away in the distance and been lost in the returned rhythms of the marimba players.

You have guessed already that the old fellow was the one I had first been attracted to: he of the noble face and white locks to the shoulder, he beside whom I had made my seat. Presently I addressed him softly.

"The wolf calls to you, *señor*. What does he say?"

He looked sharply at me. He was certainly startled, but I also detected what might have been gratitude in the old eyes. "You do not jest, *señor*? You do not ridicule me?"

"But of course not, *viejo,* old one. I sympathize. I am in accord. I would hear what you may have to tell me."

He nodded and returned to what I thought was his endless gazing into the embers of the fire. But I had not lost him, nor he his memories.

"I was once young," he began, "even as they who click the heel and stamp the boot there where the music sounds. Rich I was in land and sheep and cattle. For wife I had one of great beauty and God-given graces. The good Christ had seen fit, as well, to bless us with a beautiful son. To this *hijo* belonged our total lives. He was the light that lit the pathways of our existence. Do you understand?"

"But of course." I bowed. "Please to continue."

"Almost daily was this son in my company, from his first birthday onward. Always was he guarded with extreme caution lest harm befall him. You see, it had befallen that, in his birth, some damage was done. My wife could bear no other child. Thus in the boy we dwelled to a degree not healthy. Eventually such bondage as we forced upon the poor little lad became unbearable to him. He longed, just once, to wander forth without the guard of *vaqueros* that followed me, as I followed him.

" 'Please, *Padre,*' he would beg of me. '*Por favor,* only this one time allow me to see the land by myself. There is something out there that seems to call to me, and I want to

212

go and find out what it is."

The old man paused, shaking his silvered head.

"You will recognize this was strange talk coming from a little boy of but a few summers' age. But I was not old and wise, then, and I answered the lad impetuously and without good reason told him, no. The springtime softened into the summer, and those brief golden days of August came and went . . . like heat lightning, and like our youth, splendid and exciting, yet also strangely muffled and . . . oh! . . . so very swift and soon gone . . . and after that came the autumn and the red leaves and the yellow on the slopes and in the river bottoms. Soon the first fall of snow lay on the shoulders of El Trueno, mantling his palisades to the first flats and benches above the valleys.

"One day toward the fall of evening my little son was not to be found. It was full starlight when we discovered upon one of the higher flats, amid the juniper and greasewood, his small tracks, dim and lonely, leading off through the thin snowfall up the north slope of El Trueno. As my *vaqueros* set off urgently pursuing this faint trail, slowed, of course, by the darkness and by the treacherous footing for their horses, the penetrating scream of the panther was heard from above us and in the direction those tiny footprints led. And more. Even as my men and I exchanged fearful glances at this first dread sound, it was overlain by a second cry, far more compelling than that of the panther. It was *el grito del lobo,* the marrow-freezing hunger cry of the great gray timber wolf.

"Esteban Chavez, my *mayordomo,* looked at me. '*El lobo llama,*' he said. 'I am afraid. I think he calls to us.'

" 'Lead on, Esteban,' I replied.

"He gave me a sorrowing glance. The men did the same. But they put spurs to mounts and went on up the icy slope because they loved me and my small son.

"We came to a very dangerous switchback in the trail, then a topping-out place, studded with boulders and scrub-like pines. There before our eyes lay the signs of disaster. The broad paw of the panther showed in the snow, joining the track of my son. Chavez knew this particular panther. It had had the two central toes of the left forefoot cut off by one of our traps, and Chavez and the men called this great cat La Sombra, The Shadow. The story told around the *campos* of our sheep and cattle herdsmen was that this animal was a female bigger than any male, and more . . . that she was not of the pure mountain lion blood, such as the panthers we knew and called pumas, but rather had for a sire some wandering Mexican jaguar male, up here in the Sangres, God knows how, on a wanderlust of hunger. This La Sombra, then, was not as other pumas, which will not harm man, not even his children or his woman. She was a killer of men and had murdered three of my own *pastores*, two of them only young boys."

Again the old man paused, his memory reaching back along the dim track of time.

"I became as one possessed," he resumed. "I threw all caution to the freezing winds and raced along the difficult trail. Suddenly the final spark of my hope was plunged out. There, before my eyes, a third track joined the previous two. I stared down in disbelief at the great, splay-footed mark of El Lobo. We called him only that, El Lobo . . . *The* Wolf. And we said it that way, marking a line under the El with our tongue. All knew which wolf was meant...El Lobo, the most dreaded animal in New Mexico. Some said even that he had been feared when Oñate and Díaz and Pedro Alvarado rode here, calling all this land New Spain. Some will say this. You saw their faces but a breath ago, when the great cry sobbed down from the mountain, eh?"

"*Sí, anciano.*" I nodded. "I saw them. Pray conitnue."

"As you will, *señor*. I stood but a moment hypnotizedby the mark of the huge foot in the snow. Then I raced on as before, caring not for La Sombra or El Lobo or for God or Christ or the Holy Ghost, even, but only for my son. I was in my own mind become greater than my Savior. Here was no place for the Prince of Peace. This was a time for the Avenger, and I was that one. My rifle was ready, my knife and my pistol, too. With my bare hands I would have attacked either beast, or both. Hope was dead, but revenge was mine. In my madness I forged far ahead of my followers, in this manner coming first upon the tragedy.

"The way that the panther's tracks read in the snow, I knew that I stood behind the very boulder from which the bestial cat had hurled herself upon my son. I lunged beyond the fatal rock, dreading to have my worst fears confirmed, yet insane with vengeance.

"*Señor,* you will be hard-pressed to accept it. Rounding that great stone, I fell headlong over a huddled mass, measuring my length on the trail beyond. Sitting up, I beheld the monster carcass of La Sombra, rigid in that death which for her was but an experience she had meted out to countless pitiful others. Her enormous, whiskered head was thrown aside and lay at a grotesque angle. The white throat ruff was dyed crimson, the throat itself ripped open earbase to earbase."

"El Lobo?" I interjected quietly.

"The same, *señor*. In the one fearsome strike, he had smashed her down as lightning rives the mighty pine. But why, *señor?* That is what had Esteban Chavez and my men staring about into the black night and muttering as they crossed themselves.

"We scratched the mountainside for any sign of my son.

Nothing was discovered until, hidden in the sheltered bottom of a small *cañada* . . . you know, *señor,* a little cleft or rift in the mountain's flank . . . I found a thing that set the short hairs at the nape of my neck to bristling. There in the starlight were the marks of El Lobo's great splayed paws with the tiny footprints of my lost son, *moving side by side.* And that is the way those tracks disappeared into the darkness down the mountain's wild and desolate slope."

I let the old man pause to think his own thoughts. I did not dare to break the slender thread that was leading him back through the years. Presently he sighed deeply and returned to those misty times.

"Long and weary was the trailing through that night," he said. "My men were several times at the edge of exhaustion, at the rebel's point of turning back. But, as I, they loved the boy. We staggered on, our horses now behind us, led by their bridles, the way too steep and treacherous for them to bear us. Dawn found us at our trail's end. And, yes, I see that you have guessed it . . . the trail brought up sharply at the very door of my own great *hacienda.* From that place, the giant tracks of the wolf faded back into the fastness of El Trueno.

"Frantically, I rushed into my house, only to be met and silenced by my *mozos* and my women, who informed me that the boy had been snugly in his bed and sleeping these three hours!"

The old man frowned, moving his head uncertainly.

"The boy had simply come out of the blackest part of the dawn, saying he was tired and wanted to go to his bed. He seemed in no way disturbed by his harrowing experience. The following day, however, we noted an odd reluctance on his part to discuss, in any way, the adventure. That he had been with the wolf we could determine. He made several references to the 'big gray dog,' and we found upon his garments a

216

great quantity of the black-tipped silver guard hairs of the timber wolf, as though, indeed, the great brute and my son may have lain down together to rest upon the trail at a point during their remarkable journey.

"Some time later the boy's behavior became more marked in its strangeness. We called in the priest, but he could gain no more from my son than could we, his parents and protectors. I have never since that day been the child of Mother Church that once I was. It seemed to me that here we were dealing with some very definite work of Lucifer, yet this bumbling *padre* could achieve no more than to thumb his beads and implore the saints to send a sign by which he might know his way in the matter. Ah, what good is a God who will not better instruct his minions than that? Had I such a *mozo* or *peón* or *vaquero*, I would discharge him or at least restrict his supply of *chiles* and *frijoles*. Well, I have wandered. Excuse me!"

"It is nothing," I assured him. "All of these thoughts will pass through the mind in the remembering. I agree with you about priests. They eat too well. As you know, I am of the Faith, but I don't trust all these *padres*. I've known the sort you speak of. They ought to have been cart drivers, or charcoal burners, or, again, *muleteros*, or donkey women."

This pleased him fleetingly.

"Yes, they know more of boot soles than of human souls. In any event, the boy became more and more peculiar. He was to be found from time to time in the extreme cold of the patio . . . winter was upon us now . . . clad only in his night clothes gazing away toward the mountain, his face lacking all mortal animation. When I questioned him somewhat sternly about these midnight forays, he only replied softly . . . 'He is calling me, Father. Cannot you hear him up there upon the mountain?'

" 'Who is calling?' I demanded sharply, and he answered me, still looking far away . . . *El lobo que llora,* the wolf that cries.'

"It was hopeless . . . and very frightening. Each night the chill wail would come sobbing down from the heights of El Trueno. Sometimes the others of us could hear it, and sometimes we could not. But the boy heard it always.

"We attempted every device. Other priests were sent in from afar, even a bishop from Coahuila. Doctors we brought in from Socorro, Santa Fé, and even Las Cruces. What use? They charged us much money and left the boy no better. I have since felt about doctors as I do about *padres.* They should all have been carpenters, like the father of Jesus."

This was the last pause now. One sensed it.

"Well, *señor,* you have been patient. It was on an eternally damned night, brief weeks later, that my son disappeared for the final time. But this time he did not leave alone. Leading from the door of my *hacienda,* clearly imprinted on the newly fallen snow, side by side with those small marks of my son's tiny feet, were the great pad marks of the wolf.

"We searched the mountain again the whole night through, but you know the end, already, of this story. We did not find the boy. We did not find the wolf. Their trail faded into nothingness on the upper slopes of Thunder Mountain. The night was clear. The starlight blazing bright at the great height. Yet the tracks disappeared as if into the still black air.

"Nor did we ever find my son, *señor.* Stories there were, and continued to be . . . small, frozen bodies found, tiny human skeletons revealed by the summer thaw high on the mountain, but always no real proof, always the body or the bones were gone when my riders and I came up to where they had been seen.

"After a certain time, my proud spirit died. My mind wandered, and my riches with it. Even my name was forgotten. It still is forgotten. These happy ones in this room do not remember me, only my story.

"It is as well. Do you know what night it was upon which the boy last left me, the night we found the wolf tracks leading him away from that door beyond the dancers there? It was on the same night as this present one, *señor*, the same night and in this very *hacienda*, then mine, that it happened. Do you wonder, now, that I start up when El Lobo calls upon the mountain? Do you wonder that I hold my hand to my ear, listening to hear if it is my name he calls at last? Well, *señor*, the time of waiting is done. Tonight I heard my name. I am content, my friend. Already it grows overlong since I have seen my little son. It will be a glad meeting on the far mountain. Remember that. Let there be no sadness, now, when the wolf has called again."

I started to say something to him, as his words trailed off, but my own words never left my lips. A log dislodged in the fireplace, sending up a shower of sparks. The noise of the revelers grew unaccountably quiet. I shook myself to ward off a sensation of creeping cold, or of a frosty draft of air. I even looked to see if some overheated dancers had opened the great oaken door of the *hacienda*. They had not.

Yet, suddenly, the merrymakers froze in their positions. A popping ember echoed in the stillness. From high above an eerily beautiful wolf howl sounded on Thunder Mountain. At the first notes of the call, the old man by my side glanced upward in the direction of El Trueno. But as the final strains sobbed from the heights, he was no longer looking toward the mountain. He was leaning back with a gentle smile of peace, and I realized the gallant soul had fled. There remained, however, one element of that departure that puzzled me. It was a thing I had to make sure of in my own mind, for the sake of my own peace.

I went quickly to the oaken door of the *hacienda*. When no one was watching, I opened it and stepped outside. A new snow was falling. It lay all about the ranch yard, innocent of disturbance except for a singular distinct impression upon its starlit surface. From the *hacienda*'s doorstep, stretching away from it into the winter darkness toward the waiting midnight snows of El Trueno lay three sets of footprints. One set was those of a very old man, one those of a very young lad, and one those of a larger American timber wolf than I had ever seen.

Even as I stared at the ghostly footprints of the three companions, their track marks were beginning to fade beneath the increasing fall of the snow. When I returned to the big room of the *hacienda* and was told the old man had, indeed, passed on, I went again to the oaken door and looked out into the night.

The tracks were gone. The snow beyond the ancient doorstep lay clean of any mark, and I never repeated this story, then or since.

Many winters afterward, as I studied a letter of congratulations addressed to me by my colleagues of the government biological survey, I had cause to think once more of my peculiar experience at Don Gaspar's *hacienda*. The government letter concerne dmy lifelong work in the habits of the Western timber wolf. It expressed particular praise for my paper describing all the known calls and cries of the animal, and, of course, it was this latter fact that returned my memory to the Agua Piedra Ranch and the snow-shrouded ramparts of El Trueno.

Ah, wait. Do not smile understandingly and turn away, young friends. Consider this matter. In spite of the position of authority granted me by my colleagues in the study of the American wolf, I have never succeeded in identifying the species that uttered the incredibly sad and eerie lament that swept the winter air over Don Gaspar's *hacienda* that Christmas night so long ago.

Honors and letters from wise men do not make a man wise. The great animal whose tracks I saw leading toward El Trueno, and whose howl I heard wafting down from that snowy peak, remains for me, as for the most ignorant *peón* on the slopes of the Agua Piedra—the Ghost Wolf of Thunder Mountain.

CUSTER

Will Henry

Hated by the Indians, feared by his own men, George Armstrong Custer will stop at nothing in his quest for personal glory. But the daring leader of the illustrious 7th Cavalry will find his most lasting fame in his final defeat— the Indians' greatest victory—at the Little Big Horn. Now, combined for the first time in a single volume, here are Will Henry's two novels of Custer's life: *Yellow Hair,* the story of Custer as a brash, young General; and *Custer's Last Stand,* the tale of his tragic fate. In these classic novels, the West's most legendary figure is brought to life by its finest storyteller.

____4569-9 $5.50 US/$6.50 CAN

ALIAS BUTCH CASSIDY

No one would make a more unlikely outlaw than young George LeRoy Parker, grandson of a Mormon bishop. But at sixteen Parker throws in with Mike Cassidy, a shrewd old bandit who sees something in the boy nobody else does—the courage of a cougar and the heart of a renegade. Old Mike teaches the kid everything he knows, and before he is done there is no outlaw more feared, hunted, or idolized than George LeRoy Parker. . . .

___4516-8 $4.50 US/$5.50 CAN